ROGUE Q

EROTIC ADVENTURE OF THE PRINCESS OF GOTHAM

WRITTEN BY

JOHN JAYNESIS

Published by: **WINTER FIELD PUBLISHING**

Copyright © 2023 by Winter Field Publishing Inc.

All rights reserved. This book or any portion thereof may not be reproduced or used in any manner whatsoever without the express written permission of the publisher except for the use of brief quotations in a book review.

Printed in the United States of America

First Printing, 2020

ISBN: 9798389384934

Book Central Inc.

51 S Cicero Ave

Matteson, IL 60443, USA

lifeisg00d@bookcentral. org

CONTENTS

PART 1 ....**9**
    CHAPTER 01 11
    CHAPTER 02 30

PART 2 ....**46**
    CHAPTER 01 48
    CHAPTER 02 175
    CHAPTER 03 193
    CHAPTER 04 203
    CHAPTER 05 231
    CHAPTER 06 251

PART 3 ....**282**
    CHAPTER 01 284

AUTHOR NOTE..**302**

PART 1

HARLEY QUINN

GONE ROGUE

CHAPTER 01

Harley Quinn was now officially single and a solo villain aiming for the big leagues. Dumping Joker's ass and wrecking his place was the most liberating feeling she had ever felt in her life. Now she felt really stupid for not following Ivy's advice earlier. It felt nice not being that pasty asshole's punching bag and scapegoat for once. She felt even stupider for not realizing that she was basically the white guy whose black friends leave behind to handle the police while they make their getaway.

But that was all in the past now. Harley Quinn was now her own woman and she was going to usurp Joker from his ugly ass throne and become the queen of crime in Gotham. She had a new look, new digs and a new signature weapon that would make even Batman pause (or at least Robin after taking a nice, hard swing at that little brat's face. Have fun getting that nose realigned Round Robin!), and she had the experience thanks to hanging around Joker for all those years.

However there were several things keeping her from achieving that dream, namely that she didn't have her own crew. Ivy didn't count as she was sort of her supervillain supervisor/moral support and had her own little crew of Gotham orphans and sentient plants backing her up. So Harley had to go on a little recruitment drive, which was hard to do in Gotham considering that while there were plenty of villains and criminal metahumans to choose them, the stark majority of them were complete shit and a number of the truly good ones were already snatched up by existing villains and crime lords.

Her only lead (thanks to the efforts of Fat Tony who totally wasn't fat) was a metahuman who lived in the "better" part of Crime Alley in Gotham. The guy's name was Lupa, and while he wasn't an outright villain, he had a reputation of beating the shit out of thugs and others metas starting things in his part of town, as he really didn't want any part of the Bat Family sniffing about his turf. Harley heard a lot of good things about Lupa, from him being an okay guy to getting the job done when the situation called for it.

Lupa was also a father to a little girl...and he was also a wolfman. A very angry wolfman.

"Um...hi!" Harley said to the massive wolfman before her. It wasn't often that Harley was nervous in front of other people but this guy certainly made her feel like a beta. "My name is Harley

Quinn, you know former sidekick of Joker and all that, and I'm here to offer you the job opportunity of a lifetime!"

Lupa was sitting on his incredibly comfortable and stylish couch looking at Harley without an ounce of interest in her sales pitch. The man was tall, around eight feet in height and incredibly muscular, though not to the degree that he'd look obscene. His body was covered in pristine white fur and his head was that of a wolf's head, with dark amber gold eyes that watched her every move. Harley admitted that he was a fine male specimen, given that he was going shirtless at the moment, and his arms were crossed in front of his muscular chest that she totally wanted to.

"Ouch!" Harley jumped at the bite on her calf and she glared down at the little girl trying to nom on her leg.

"Selene, please don't try to eat our guest." Lupa said in a deep, baritone voice that made Harley shiver. Holy damn this guy sounded fine! "I haven't given the order to attack yet."

Selene was Lupa's five-year-old daughter, also a meta but could switch between her human and wolf forms like an actual werewolf. She was a cute little thing, with big blue eyes and short curly brown hair, but acted like a fucking guard dog when

Lupa was conducting his "business" with people. Heeding her father's orders, Selene backed off, but not before sending Harley a defensive glare as she scampered off to parts unknown.

"As I was saying," Harley cleared her throat. "I've just recently broken away from Joker, shocking I know, and now I'm planning on taking over that grinning fuck's place at the top of Gotham's villain food chain."

"And to do that, you need a crew." Lupa said.

"And to do that I need—wait, how'd you know?" Harley blinked.

"I saw your callout for henchmen and fellow villains to join your crew online." Lupa answered. "Word to the wise, don't put up a call for help on Craigslist. No one uses that anymore."

Harley had the decency to blush at being found out. "Right, got it."

"If you really know about me, then you know that I don't get involved with Gotham's stupid hero/villain power plays. Penguin tried to get me and I turned him into a turkey. Black Mask tried to recruit me and I beat him to death with his own skull. I gave Scarecrow a phobia of dogs and broke Joker's legs before making him dance at my daughter's birthday party."

"Haha, I remember that." Harley laughed at the memory. "Man, I had a good laugh at that party."

"And when the Batman came knocking, I sicked my little girl on the boy wonder and she put his ass in the hospital for several weeks while I gave Batman the Bane treatment." At this point, Lupa had gotten up from the couch and was slowly stalking towards Harley, who was nervously backing up until her back hit the wall. The modern werewolf towered over her smaller, curvy form but Harley did her best not to look nervous before him. "What exactly do you, Joker's former squeeze and a rookie solo villain with little to no resources of her own, have to offer me?"

Harley knew she was walking on thin ice at this point, and Lupa made some really great points. Villains stronger and scarier than her had tried to get him to join them only to be turned away. She was on a level even lesser than them and she barely had a good grasp on how to make it up in the underworld. So, with little choice left, Harley gave him the only thing a women like her had in this situation.

"I'll let you fuck me."

Lupa blinked, his eyes wide. Her sudden and very unexpected reply caught him off guard, which was rare for a seasoned warrior like him. "I'm...I'm sorry, what did you say?"

"I said," Harley's red lips slowly spread into a grin. "I'll let you fuck me. I don't have a lot of money, or a good track record, but I do have what the good lord gave me, and that's an above average rack and the tightest ass this side of Gotham. Join me and I'll let you do whatever you want with me."

Lupa's eyes unconsciously roamed down her body. Harley was clad in her new signature outfit, a skimpy red and black corset that showcased her plump cleavage and toned stomach, and tight booty shorts that hugged her ass like second skin with matching thigh-high socks and sneakers. Certainly an improvement over her old jester costume, which while sexy in its own way, was a bit outdated at this point. He looked up at Harley's face and saw her smirk, knowing she had him.

"You sound so confident that you have me." Lupa said, regaining his balance. "Do you honestly expect me to believe that you're offering sex for my services?"

"Wanna a test run?" Harley asked coyly. "I've been known to give good head."

Lupa grinned and crossed his arms over his chest. "Go right ahead. I want to see how serious you are about this."

A short time later, Lupa found himself in his bedroom, sitting on the edge of his bed with Harley Quinn on her knees before him with his throbbing canine cock currently residing snugly between her lips.

Harley moaned as she worked her head up and down along his cock. She was moving on autopilot at this point, her mind having gone blank since she first caught sight of that juicy, aching cock as it was shoved into her face. She didn't care about anything else other than pure lust, eagerly shoving down and giving a sloppy, messy, wet, loud sucking to the big dick in front of her. pretending she was anything else would have been an embarrassing lie to herself, and she was much better off just indulging aggressive in the chance to slobber all over a big cock and let herself go, rocking her head back and forth as Lupa's stead thrusts met her face, pushed deep into her mouth and showed Harley the good time she needed.

Pushing down deep and shamelessly rocking her head along the cock, Harley embrace a special kind of shamelessness. It was rare that she ever got to enjoy herself like this. This was probably the best dick she's ever sucked in her career as a supervillain, and considering the only guy she's fucked was Joker, that wasn't saying much. Even beating the shit out of Joker with her bare hands paled in comparison to the thick, juicy cock between her lips. Any pretense of this being an interview went out the window as she moved back and forth along the shaft.

Louder and faster she sucked, making sure her head was moving in broad motions each time, covering plenty of area on the thick cock before her. There was so much dick to handle and the last thing Harley wanted was to leave any of it unsucked, to half-ass this amazing treat. The big, furry hand grabbing the back of her head urged her in tighter still, and she moaned louder around the cock. Lupa was surprisingly gentle with her despite his growing arousal and bestial urges.

Lupa sat there, holding tightly onto the woman as she worked along his cock, his hand guiding the back of her head further down with eager suggestions. He could not speak at this point, driven into a feral state of pure need right now, something he rarely experienced with all but the tightest and most experienced whores that were willing to lay with him. This pale-skinned nutjob clearly knew what the hell she was doing.

Harley was ready to draw this out as long as she could, and the eager bobbing of her head seemed to only grow quicker as her needy embrace of this lust wound her up hotter and hotter still. This all felt so right to Harley, and she happily sucked that cock right up to the edge of his orgasm, and Lupa grew more tense, more vocal, a growl rumbling in his throat and his cock twitched in her hot mouth.

Undeterred and unafraid, Harley welcomed the release, welcomed his utter unwinding as he came, and he came hard. Lupa's cock erupted, pumping hot shots of gooey, creamy seed deep into her mouth and overwhelming her with the sweet flood of cum to swallow down. Lupa's virile cock erupted with so much that Harley couldn't hold onto it all, cum spilling from her lips as she was fed more than she could handle, but she took it well, moaning and gulping down mouthfuls of hot, creamy wolfman spunk to the best of her ability, all while staring with glimmering, loving eyes up at him.

Once he was done cumming, Harley slid his cock from her lips and leaned back, gulping the cum down and grinning at him. "How's that? You up for some more?"

Lupa said nothing, though his hungry gaze and rough panting showed that he wanted more from her. He roughly pulled her to her feet and reached down to her corset, ripping it in half and letting her large tits bounce free to his hungry gaze. Harley yelped and giggled as she was pushed onto the bed, and Lupa scrambled after her, the hulking mess of fur and muscle straddling her chest and showing off the raw size difference between them as he settled his thick, aching cock down between her breasts, so impatient and eager that he didn't even wait for her to press her breasts together and close them around his cock to begin thrusting.

Harley giggled and whined as she felt him atop her, so strong and proud, thrusting away before she was even prepared to handle him. "That's it, fuck me." She moaned, relishing the depraved excitement that came from having the furry beast fucking her tits. She pressed them tightly together around his cock, holding them steady as she prepared herself for what was to come. His proud cock prodded her chin and her lips at the furthest reaches of his thrusts, and as she stuck her tongue out, Harley was able to lick at the head and offer it some more pleasure as she readied herself to be use and fucked as hard as she possibly could be.

"Oh boy, you're much better than my pasty-faced ex-boss." arley moaned. She didn't even care that her corset was torn in half, she'd gladly let him walk her through the streets naked if she got to get fucked like this every day.

Eager thrusts into the softness of Harley's plush tits had Lupa growling in excitement, his powerful, towering body leaning forward clutching at the bed for balance as he rocked back and forth with the kind of rawness and fervor he rarely felt during sex. The soft embrace of her breasts around his cock, the incredible warmth of being so close into her chest and feeling her body heat around him, on top of that incredibly sex and crazy smile she was giving him now made him go harder and faster into her chest.

Starting him off with her mouth and then moving onto her tits wasn't doing much to get Harley off, but she was more than happy to indulge in his appetites as she marveled at his cock thrusting forward, especially from the angle she was looking at as it emerged from her cleavage. The indulgence of getting titfucked was doing wonderful things between her legs, getting her all hot and bothered as she squirmed on the bed, legs rubbing together and the throbbing, aching tension building up inside her getting stronger and stronger.

"I never thought you'd be this intense." She panted, biting her lip as she stared up at him, adoring everything about this man as he used her without hesitation.

Lupa wasn't listening. All he was concerned about was the need to fuck, and fuck he did, ponding forward and subjecting Harley to the intensity that kept her writing and moaning. He swatted away her hands and grabbed hold of her chest to pound forward himself, groping and squeezing at her plump breasts as he himself felt the need to fuck harder and better, to put her through the worst of what he could muster in the midst of his lusty heights.

"Fuck them harder." Harley moaned, relishing the delight of being used and fucked so deep and hard. "Come on, blow it all over my face. Cum on me, do it!"

Fortunately for Harley, Lupa was loving her demands and her desperation, relishing in her needy whines and the shameless thrills that she accepted deep within her. He thrust forward harder and faster, working up a feverish and desperate pace that refused to slow itself down until finally he was done, howling in ecstasy as he came, cock twitching as he pulled back and blew a massive load all over her. Cum blasted her chest, up along her neck, and onto her face, streaking along her cheek, into her mouth and even getting into her hair. Harley whined and shuddered, cumming herself as she happily gulped down the cum in her mouth, rubbing his white seed into her pale skin.

Harley panted heavily, staring at Lupa as he rose, remaining steady as his body heaved with powerful breaths, and his inexhaustible cock stood completely rigid, ready for more and refusing to quit. "I hope you got more in the tank for the main event." She said, hopeful and excited. He fucked her mouth, fucked her tits, and now she was ready for one last go in her main hole.

Harley got what she wanted as Lupa reached for her, grabbing hold of her body and pulling her to the edge of the bed, rolling her so quickly she barely had time to scramble onto all fours for him. She whined as he tore off her shorts and snapped her thong like a piece of paper. Harley ignored the fact that her only outfit was now in shreds on the floor and just enjoyed the moment for what it was.

She felt that twitching, aching cock push up against her sopping wet twat, and her hips shivered in anticipation. She looked over her shoulder, face still streaked with cum, and said, "Fuck me."

With a mighty howl, Lupa shoved his cock a few inches into Harley and began to fuck her with deep, excited strokes as she screamed in ecstasy. Even if he wasn't that deep into her, the girth of his meaty cock was enough to make her twist. Her pale cheeks reddened and she gasped and moaned under the harshness of it, shaking and twisting as the ecstasy set in. This was better than she ever imagined!

"I should have expected you to want to f-f-fuck me do-doggy-style!" Harley moaned, stumbling over her words as the powerful thrusts into her needy pussy made her sing out with excitement. The pleasure was overwhelming, intense, and she ached with elation as she felt it all take her. Each thrust shook her, made her dangling breasts heave, almost shoving her face into the extremely soft pillows under her. Lupa was a mess of primal hungers waiting to be unleashed and she fucking loved it!

He'd been patient in enjoying her mouth, gotten playful and aggressive in fucking her tits, but when it came to the snug, tight pussy wrapped around his cock, hot and wet, he couldn't help himself. Her desperate snatch almost pulled him in, and he just lost it. Back and forth he hammered with primal, depraved hunger, and Harley was as loud as she could be in the raw enjoyment of that fact. Each thrust pushed in deeper, until his cock was buried all the way inside her, until she felt his swollen, bulbous knot pressing against her pussy lips with each thrust.

With the throbbing wolfman cock inside her, Harley was in heaven, fingers digging into the sheets as she held herself steady, loving the heavy body thrusting into her, the strong hands that refused to let go of her wide hips as he showed her his most brutal pounding. Lupa fucked her with the intent to breed, and Harley was almost certain that there was no real danger of being bred in the heated midst of it all, but it was hot to be fucked like this, pounded into submission like the whore she was. Fuck Joker's tiny dick, THIS was where it was at!

"Holy shit, this is so much better than Joker!" Harley screamed, head thrown back as she shoved against his thrusts, meeting him with all the desperation and hunger she could muster. Her body quivered, and as the meaty cock forced its way in and out of her hot pussy, she felt absolutely lost. Submitting to this hulking, furry beast, had made her realize just how much she missed out on being Joker's punching bag.

The tight, slick embrace of Harley's needy pussy was all Lupa needed, and he took her with the bubbling ferocity of an animal claiming his mate, aggressive, harsh, showing her no mercy as he thrust harshly toward orgasm. He panted heavier and harsher as he wound up, showing her his worst, pushing her to the very brink of what was left of her sanity as he staked his claim until finally, with one mighty howl, he lost himself, slamming forward into Harley so hard that he buried not only his cock into her, but his knot as well.

Harley screamed as she felt the bulb push into her, so big and thick that it locked his cock inside her just at the height of his release. His howl overwhelmed and muffled her own cries as the hot cum gushed into her welcoming womb, and all the molten seed filling her up was enough to send her crashing over the edge and into thrashing, maddened ecstasy. She screamed, whined, and even howled with primal desperation alongside the beast as her body surrendered utterly to the pleasures overtaking her. This was the best thing she ever felt in her life, and absolutely worth whoring herself out for. The orgasm that left her a thrashing mess on the bed proved so good and satisfying that her thoughts spun madly out of control and all that was left was the quivering mess of a woman that suffered the full might of Lupa's powerfucking.

She crumpled to the bed, cheek pressed against the mattress, blonde hair fallen out of her pigtails as she lay there shuddering in ecstasy. The knot locked Lupa's wolf cock inside of her pussy, leaving her full and reminded with each passing second that he wasn't done with her. It was highly possible that once he pulled out of her, she would only get rolled over and fucked again.

"So..." Harley panted, barely able to see thanks to the tears in her eyes from cumming so hard. "How about that deal?"

She felt Lupa's cock shudder inside her, earning another moan, before he resting his body atop hers. "Fine, I'll join you. If I can get this ass all to myself, I'm willing to help you get into the big leagues."

Harley's red lips widened into that familiar crazed grin as she tightened her cunt on Lupa's throbbing dick. "I think I'm there already."

"...That was a terrible joke." He grumbled.

"We're going to get along swimmingly!" She cackled.

CHAPTER 02

6MONTHS LATER, EARTH, USA, GOTHAM

Grey rose gasping for air from the Gotham docks. He silently treads water and observed the groups of men loading and unloading crates from one boat to another. His vision blurred and the colour melted away as he saw the same men but in the day opening the crates and finding guns inside. He recognized the city as Metropolis. Grey shook his head and swam over to the dock. He climbed onto the pier and caught his breath, grinning to himself. He loved the city at night. His vision went gray as he looked up to see fists and boots rain down on him. Shaking his head he quickly rolled forward as a boot cracked the board he had been kneeling on. He turned and fired a custom built weapon he had under his jacket. The single barrel fired a plastic slug that safe house into a man's stomach. The man flew backwards with audible cracks as his ribs broke from the slug and landed behind his two friends. Both of the thugs looked up as Grey stood and backed away. The gun was only single shot and he could reload but that was more than enough time for the two thugs to charge him and kill him. Suddenly a shadow fell behind the men and pulled a thug backwards onto the floor and kicked the second one in the head. They both crumpled on the ground. The shadow rose, as Grey reloaded and took in the sight of the Batman.

"How did you find these men," Batman said in his monotone voice "I had them under surveillance".

"Precognition" Grey stated holstering his weapon "I saw the semen in a cafe and then ta da vision".

Batman remained motionless but a twitch passed across his face. "How did you acquire the visions?"

"Well" Grey began "I woke up in the streets with memories of big red men yelling about extinction and my responsibilities, they said something about my failures" Grey shrugged as he walked to the edge of the pier and looked at the men smuggling across the water "I couldn't remember anything, I started helping people, tracking down missing persons".

"Your ... visions" Batman spoke, moving to stand beside Grey on the pier "Can you see anyone?"

"Sure, it's focused around me but if I look for someone I can find them in a few days."

"I need your help tracking someone down, Harley Quinn"

"Really" Grey exclaimed looking up at the Bat "Wow high profile case, why do you need me?"

"She's gone underground, planning a breakout at Arkham, I can't track what doesn't move" Batman stated and turned and shot a grappling line "Find her and tell me where she is, here next week"

Grey looked up as The Bat scaled the side of the building and glided towards the smugglers over the water.

THREE DAYS LATER…

Grey looked out of the window across the street and counted the men leaving the building. One, two, three and then four men left, looking both ways nervously and drove off in a van. This was his chance. Finding Harley had been easy, incredibly easy actually and he had spent the last six days staking out one of her hideouts. Yesterday Harleys men had left and moved goods across town in four pickup trucks. It seems that today would be no exception. Grey checked his watch. 22:00. He had about four and a half hours before they would return and after seeing what would happen after getting caught in a vision, they were all carrying guns. He looked in the mirror, a tall average man with gray eyes wearing a navy v-neck, gray cargo jeans, and a black overcoat. Grey opened the door, peered to the side to check the van was gone and crossed the road. Grey jiggled the door finding it locked and brought out a switch knife and broke off the rusted lock. Before he was an abandoned warehouse with old crates and furniture. Running along the sides and crisscrossing above the room was metal catwalks. Grey slid into the room and moved through the shadows.

"BOYS is that you?" A feminine voice called through the building.

Grey moved across the room hugging the wall and going from cover to cover. He watched Harley enter the room wearing black fishnet tights, blue and red sparkly booty shorts and a tight white t-shirt. Her white hair was in two ponytails on either side of her head, one red and one blue. Grey climbed up an old fridge to perch on the catwalk overlooking the storage room.

"Whoever's out there better come out or I'll smash their face in" Harley warned, her wide eyes circling the room. "I don't wanna hurt ya so just come out and say hi, I won't bite"

Grey watched her move through the room, circling with a baseball bat. She licked her lips at the thought of having some fun with the intruder. God, she was bored. Waiting around for Mister J's contacts to break him out and trying not to raise the attention of the numerous vigilantes in Gotham took patience, something that Harley didn't have a lot of. Additionally, she was horny. Subconsciously she started to massage her breast through her t-shirt. With only four meatheads to stare at she had been stewing in her room fingering herself to orgasm after orgasm but she needed something, else.

Grey dropped down behind her silently and appraised her perky ass and long legs.

"Harley" He stated, moving a step back out of range of the baseball bat that swung towards him.

"Whatcha doing here" Harley demanded staring Grey down.

"Just here to share some information" Grey casually said putting his hands in his pockets and pacing back and forth "About how the Bat has put me on your trail". Grey noticed the spark in Harley's face and continued "I would be willing to lie or even deceive the Batman for a better deal".

"Oh well why didn't you say so" Harley exclaimed straight up. "Let's talk in my office, you first" Harley gestured to a small side room.

Grey saw himself being battered with the bat as soon as he turned his back to her but had trapped himself into a conversation with her. "No, you first" Grey replied, "I insist".

"Sure thing follows me," Harley said swaying her hips from side to side.

Inside was a bed, a couch and a desk with a leather office chair. Harley gestured to the couch and watched Grey sit down and take off his coat.

"I'll just get us a drink m'kay" Harley drawled turning away towards the desk and started pouring two shots. Fuck fuck fuck she thought. Mister J was gonna kill her if the escape was ruined. And how did this guy find out where her safehouse was. The only sure thing to do was kill him. She turned and saw him staring at her ass and winked at him. Well, this should be fun she thought.

Grey watched her bend over to pick up the bottle and admired her smooth legs in those tights. He really had no reason to stay any longer, he had all the intel he needed to report back to Batman but for some reason, he was still sitting there and was now going to share a drink with Harley Quinn of all people. His eyes roamed her body as he thought fuck Batman I'll bring him Harley in person. He took off his coat and looked up to see her wink at him and thought, this should be fun, as Harley turned with the drinks.

"Here ya go," Harley said handing Grey his drink and sitting down on the couch with him. She crossed her legs and rubbed one up against Grey and lowered her head at him and whispered: "drink up". Grey tilted his head back and drank it down feeling the burn of the whiskey on the back of his throat. He felt Harley's hand start to stroke his arm and her leg rub against his as she leaned in and slowly exhaled onto his lips. Grey leaned forward and gasped as Harley squeezed his cock and sucked his neck. "Wow, that's uh wow" Grey gasped as Harley giggled into his neck. He suddenly saw himself being stabbed repeatedly in the chest with Harley on top of him. "Hey, I didn't squeeze you that hard did I?" Harley said staring at Grey before sucking his neck and moving down to his collarbone. "No just god your tongue" Grey stuttered trying to concentrate, where was her knife!?!

"Mmmmm tell me how good it feels baby" Harley whispered before standing up. She pushed Grey down onto his back so he was sitting down on the couch leaning back before she swung a leg over him and lifting off his shirt. She began bucking her hips against him while biting his ear. Greys' hand roamed her back before settling at her ass squeezing it and pulling her in with her every movement of her hips. She stopped her kissing to whisper in his ear "I'm gonna make you feel so good" and leaned over him, smothering his face in her t-shirt covered tits. Grey moaned into the tight fabric and suddenly realized she was trying to reach for something behind the couch. Grey wrapped his arms around Harley and flung her down onto the couch and moved on top of her shoving his tongue into her mouth. Out the corner of his eye, he saw the knife in Harley's hand skid across the floor and under the desk. He smiled as he ran his hands over her legs.

How the hell did he know?!? Harley thought her mind racing as she saw her knife slide away. She struggled to come up with a new plan fighting not only Grey's insistent hands and tongue but the growing wetness between her legs. She ran her hands down his bare back and up through his hair pulling him in closer. A groan escaped her as she felt a hardness press against her crotch. Harley moved like split oil dragging her body out from under him and stood up blowing a stray hair from his face and looked down at Greys' chest rising and falling with his fast breathing. She traced her hands down her chest lifting her breasts and sighing tilting her head back and moved her hands down her stomach to the hem of her tight white t-shirt. Slowly seductively she lifted it teasingly over her head revealing more and more of her stunning body until her chest was completely free. She tossed her shirt aside and stood before Grey, her tits standing proudly outwards with hard nipples poking out towards him, begging to be sucked.

Grey pulled her towards him, wrapping his arms around her waist pulling her closer as she leaned forwards and slowly kissed him as he leaned forwards before pushing him back with her foot. She turned around showing her tight ass in her booty shorts and backed up onto his lap and began grinding against him. As Grey started to touch her she pulled away to her desk and went into the draw. BANG Grey saw his hands covered in blood as he attempted to keep his stomach in by pushing his hands into his chest. He looked up to see Harley resting a smoking gun between her heaving breasts. He shot up from his chair and ran over to Harley and yanked her shorts down and bent her over the desk, slamming the desk draw shut with a loud bang. Grey unbuckled his belt and wrenched his jeans off to reveal his iron hard cock. With one thrust he entered Harley from behind.

Harley shook with this penetration. She groaned arching her back as she adjusted to the new feel of the cock deep inside of her. She didn't even notice the sting in her hands from when the draw caught her fingers. Inside was a gold emblazoned revolver that she planned to use on Grey. She shuddered, feeling her pussy stretch to accommodate the new member inside her. She felt Greys' hands grope her ass as he pulled back slowly out of her. Harley groaned feeling it slowly pull out and tensed anticipated what was to come. Grey started thrusting.

Grey was swimming in a world of pleasure. Harley's pussy was like a velvet vice wrapped around his cock milking it as he grabbed her ass just to steady himself or he would fall on top of her. He pulled out and began thrusting back and forth slapping his body against her watching the sweat run down his naked body to mix with the sweat running down her back as she arched upwards groaning loudly. Grey felt the orgasm boiling upwards as he saw the curves oh Harleys tits bounce back and forth in front of him.

"FUUUUUUUCK!" Grey yelled spurting cum deep inside Harley's pussy and collapsed back in the chair watching as Harley lay on the desk gasping. He saw his semen drip out of her bald pussy and run down the back of her legs.

Harley looked over her shoulder at him and arched an eyebrow "Is that it?" Harley sniggered standing up and stretching.

"Harley you're just so ... tight" Grey protested sitting higher in his chair as he took in the curve of Harley's smooth hips down to her perky ass cheeks.

"You're not done yet" Harley demanded as she sauntered up to Grey, shaking her hips seductively. She knelt down next to him and slowly licked his flaccid cock right up to the tip and flicked her tongue like a snake while grinning up at him. She then moved slowly upwards craning her neck out. Closer and closer till Grey could smell the sweat on her skin and see the flecks of green in her eye. Slowly and silently she moved her lips closer and closer, parting those red fleshy lips as Grey leaned down. Then Harley dove, taking his whole erect cock in her mouth in one go, swirling her tongue around it sucking it in one glorious move.

"Oh, my god" Grey groaned at the swift and sudden envelopment of his cock, the warm, wet and insistent sucking of

Harley. And on top of it all her moans and groans, audible even with her mouth full.

"Aaaaah" Grey gasped straightening up as Harley scratched his balls with her long nails while nipping the tip of his cock. The combination of pain and pleasure was driving Grey insane as he writhed around in his chair with Harley holding his thighs while deep throating him, gagging on his cock. She straightened up and wiped her mouth of spit and swung a leg over Grey and positioned his cock as she started to rub it against her pussy, pinching her nipple. She looked down at Grey struggling with the sensory overload and laughed at him. Grey angered by this teasing grabbed her hips and brought her crashing down, spearing her with his full erection. Harley threw her head back her ponytails having come undone and her blonde hair cascading down covering her face as her mouth gaped open groaning. Grey began to thrust upwards and grabbed Harley's plump ass and pulled her down after thrusting up.

Harley pushed her hair back as she began to ride him in the chair and pulled his head forward burying it in her tits. Grey felt his control start to slip on the situation as he began to feel delirious from the lack of oxygen and a constant barrage of Harley bouncing on top of him wearing him down. As he was bombarded by her young, sweaty body he heard her laughing as she dug her nails into his back. Harley began chanting "fuck me, fuck me, fuck me, fuck me" And burying her head into Greys' shoulder whimpering "fuck me, fuck me" and bit down on his shoulder. Grey was drowning as he threw his head back. Harley was all over him. Her nails in his back. Her pussy squeezing his cock. Her hard nipples rubbing against his chest. Her face in his shoulder, biting him. And everywhere her smooth sweaty skin. "FUUUUUCK ME" Harley screamed as her pussy convulsed around his cock as an orgasm shook her body. Grey grabbed her as her body went limp from the orgasm as he continued to pump into her rag doll body and came deep inside of her.

Grey gasped fell back as he felt Harley's chest rise and fall on top of him. Harley rose up and fixed her eyes on Grey leaned forwards and kissed him and then jumped off Grey and skipped over to the bed. She got onto her hands and knees sticking her sweaty fat ass into the air.

"Won't you come and play" She pouted "Come on, for lil old me" She begged in a high pitched voice. Grey rose on his legs and strode towards her as Harley looked over her shoulder alternating with each slow swing of her ass from left to right. Grey crawled up the bed towards her and grabbed her hips and pulled her back. And began rubbing his cock up and down her wet pussy.

"Wait, do Harley a favor will ya?" She begged, pouting her lips and showing her wide eyes over her shoulder.

"What" Grey demanded as he grew increasingly horny with such a sexy women so close to him, literally rubbing her naked body against him.

"lick my ass for me," Harley said raising her ass to shake it against his chest and then down low, trapping his dick in the valley of her cheeks and began moving up and down. Grey felt the pressure in his balls beginning to stir again as his dick was squeezed between two fleshy globes. He reached forward and began fondling Harleys hanging breasts. Harley kneeled upright resting her head on his shoulder, her hair in her face and lying over her closed eye and brilliant white teeth, her gaping mouth wide open as she sighed in contentment. Grey shoved her down on the bed. Harley fell forward onto her stomach gasping at the shock. Grey grabbed her hips and pulled her ass up towards his face. He bent down and lapped his tongue against Harley's ass cheeks, covering them in saliva. Harley's body shook and shuddered as she gasped.

"Wow," Grey said straightening up and rubbing his cock over Harley's now lubricated ass. "You really seem to get off on this."

"Uh yeah, its ugh so good" Harley groaned into the bed sheets.

Grey pulled his arm back and smacked Harley's ass while he thrust his dick up and down, nestled in her fleshy ass.

"Ah yes" Harley moaned

Smack! Grey spanked her again, harder.

"Mmmmmmm yes that feels so good" Harley moaned out clawing the sheets.

Grey pulled his dick back and slapped it against Harley's asshole. He ran his hands backward and forwards on Harley's ass before squeezing her ass cheeks hard and saw the flesh spill out over the edges of his fingers. He pulled back befoe slamming forwards, thrusting his cock into Harley's asshole.

"Aaaargh" Harley screamed as she felt Grey's cock push inside her.

"Of fuck" Grey moaned as he saw his cock push inside Harley, pushing in between her tanned ass. Grey had thought Harley's pussy was tight but he felt his dick stop half way in. Grey steadied himself by planting his hand on the small of Harley's back and spread his fingers out. Grey pulled back and then thrust forward with all his might. Harley screamed out as she pushed back at the same time. Grey began pulling his dick all the way out, till just the tip remained inside and then thrust forward again. The pair began to buck and grind against each other for the next half hour until Grey felt his balls tighten. Grey pulled his cock out and threw Harley down on the bed. Harley was gasping as Grey flipped her over to her back. Harley propped herself up on her elbows and looked down at Grey, over her tanned heaving breasts and hard pink nipples. Grey shuffled up the bed and straddled her torso and rested his dick in Harley's cleavage and squeezed his dick between her fleshy globes.

"Oh yeah, baby cum all over my big soft titties" Harley moaned, rolling his balls in her hand.

Grey moaned as he felt his orgasm rise through his body. His dick jerked between his tits splattering Harley's face, chin and tits with cum. Grey fell onto his back gasping from the power of the orgasm that had shaken his body. Harley resting against Grey's chest and idly scratched Grey's chin while staring up at him. She slowly sucked his collarbone before stretching her warm sweaty body out.

Harley got up and crashed on the couch running her hands through her hair. "Phew, thanks, big boy" Harley said fixing her hair back into ponytails. Grey strolled over to a mirror on weak legs and looked down at his heaving chest and saw blood over his shoulder running down his chest. He turned around and looked over his shoulder to see claw marks on his back leaving bloody crescents.

"Fuck me," Grey said observing the war ground his body had became after only one encounter with Harley Quinn.

"I think I already did". Grey turned to see Harley lying on her stomach with her rounds ass glazed in sweat as she applied a generous amount of lipstick. She smacked her lips at him and drawled at him " Hold on I have a present for ya puddin'"

Grey's vision became awash with gray as his vision went colorless. He saw Harley whip around and blast his chest with a shotgun that was held against her naked body.

"Okay ready for round two?" Harley sang as she picked up her favorite double barrel. "I'm coming in, get ready for me to bang your brains out" Harley sang and jumped around the corner back into her office to see an empty couch, a slowly spinning chair, and an open window.

PART 2
HARLEY QUINN REMINISES ON HOW THE JOKER CHANGED HER LIFE FOREVER

CHAPTER 01

Dr. Harleen Quinzel took out a hair band and put her long blonde hair back in a ponytail. She sipped her orange juice as she sat at her desk, rummaging through her files and listening to the inmates screaming. She was a psychiatrist who had only graduated a year before. She hated working at Arkham Asylum, but her father Sgt. Mitchell Quinzel, wanted to keep an eye on her. Even at 24, she was under his thumb. He pulled enough strings and threatened enough people to make sure she couldn't get a job elsewhere.

Now, it wasn't only her career he was ruining, but her personal life as well. She began dwelling on the inevitable existence she was faced with, when a knock came on her door.

Outside stood Officer Jake Cromwell. It was well-known around Arkham that Cromwell wasn't the most ethical Gotham officer. He often took bribes from inmates and paid favors to those with power. That said, Quinzel only knew a few cops that were actually good guys, actually legit, the kind that are out there trying to make the world a better place.

"What can I do for you?" She asked.

"I got a letter for you."

It was a hand-written note. After she took it, Cromwell quickly disappeared beyond the corridor.

Come see me for some laughs. You need 'em.

She knew who J was. There was only one man brazen enough to reach out to her; if he even was a man. Known as The Joker or The Clown Prince of Gotham, he was different in every way imaginable. He had slicked back bright green hair and matching eyes that rather than hide his dark side, exemplified it. His skin was bleached white by an acid or some chemical spill. There were stories about how that occurred, but no one knew for sure. He was so different. He was a mystery.

So much of the Joker's history was unknown. Even how he became the Joker and who he was before are things nobody seems to be clear about. She knew he was a murderer, but he didn't kill out of passion or anger. He killed people for laughs. When he didn't kill them, he would drive them insane. He destroyed the minds of normal and average people with ease.

Sometimes he used chemical warfare or hypnosis, but often his words alone could control someone completely.

It was a case that any psychiatrist would want to sink their teeth into, if they could overcome their own fear. Some tried, but they always ran away. Harley, on the other hand, definitely wanted her chance at the apple. He was a legend in Gotham; a notorious, nefarious legend, but a legend

She had requested an interview months ago, but once again her father stepped in. Daddy didn't want her around The Joker, so she never was assigned to him. She got stuck with the typical criminals. Some had serious mental disorders that caused their criminal acts and then there were those who faked crazy just to be in the mental hospital instead of prison. To talk to one of the part-time offenders, while knowing that just a few rooms down was the mastermind of some of Gotham's largest hits, made her want to see him even more.

Every day, her fascination with the case grew. She would ask around and delve into any private files she could get her hands on without being caught. Whenever she was alone, she would peek and read the notes from other psychiatrists. They disliked The Joker almost as much as he despised them.

The Joker never asked to speak with psychiatrists and when he was forced to, he'd scared the hell out of them, for laughs. Harleen would hear about the antics and find herself giggling at her coworker's reaction. What did they expect? When you walk into a Lion's den, you don't think you're going to sit down and drink tea.

She swore if she ever had the chance, he wouldn't scare her in the least. She could take whatever he dealt out. She wasn't afraid of his threats or his violence or even of him. He went through 8 doctors in only six months. Currently, he didn't have an appointment with anyone, partially because no one wanted to get on his bad side. More than one doctor and guard died mysteriously after having a run-in with The Joker. One day he was assigned a 15 minute session of shock treatment. The day it was to be assessed, his psychiatrist cancelled it. The doctor's right hand was minus three fingers and all he would say was that he was hurt in an "accident" and that he reconsidered The Joker's treatment.

She read the note that Cromwell handed her again and again. She knew she couldn't deny her inquisitive instinct. Her father had the week off and her "fiancé" was working the streets.

Today would be perfect for her to see him, and something told her that the Joker already knew that.

She called his residency and spoke directly with the main guard. "This is Dr. Harleen Quinzel. I need you to write in an immediate session with resident."

"2-2-9" The guard stuttered. "Dr. Quinzel, that's the Joker"

"I'm aware. He requested me as his doctor. Now, this is on a need-to-know basis only. We will not be able to relinquish any details to anyone regarding this meeting."

"But your father…."

"My father included. If you break confidentiality, you will be fired. This would be a serious security breach and The Joker could potentially sue us for millions." She was stern in her voice but lying through her teeth.

"ummm"

"This isn't up for discussion. I don't want to have to force you out of your job for denying health care to an inmate."

"Of course, Dr. Quinzel. I will bring him down to the visiting room, immediately."

"To ensure there is no breach, the session I have with him, must be private."

"umm, with all due respect Dr. Quinzel, the Joker is the most dangerous man here. We keep him in a straight-jacket. I'll be happy to have one of our guards be in the room -"

She cut him off. "I can take care of myself and the straight-jacket will be an insurance policy. I'm on my way."

Harleen tightened her white jacket, took a brief glimpse of herself in the mirror, straightened out her glasses and refreshed her make-up. She confidently strolled down the aisle though inside, she felt her heart beating a mile a minute.

She took a few deep breaths and then turned the corner. The guard looked nervous, but reluctantly opened the door for her.

"Are you sure you don't want me here?"

"Positive."

When she walked in the room, she saw the Joker sitting on the opposite side of the table. He had his straight-jacket on but underneath instead of the orange prison uniform, he wore a tailored purple suit. One of his connections, no doubt helped him with that.

"Hello, my name is Doctor Harleen Quinzel, but I guess you know that already. I received your letter asking me to meet you."

"Yes, I promised laughs. Hopefully, I'll deliver. How are you Doctor?"

"Fine," Harleen was a bit thrown off with the niceties. "Why did you want to see me?"

"Well, because of your engagement, of course. Though, I'm not sure if I should offer congratulations or sympathies. I heard that you and Officer Redmond are getting married."

"No" she said instinctively. "I mean um well, yes. I guess, yes." Harleen looked at the diamond on her hand.

"That's some rock so why the sad face?" The Joker taunted. "Oh I know why, your daddy, the sergeant, is making you get married. That doesn't sound fair to you at all."

"Who did you hear that from?"

"And no denial!" The Joker laughed aloud. "You're not alone I don't like Redmond, either. Then again, I don't much care for your father."

"You don't like anyone in law enforcement. I know about you, Mr… Mr… what should I even call you?"

"If you ask nice, I'll let you call me Mister J."

She rolled her eyes but obliged. "May I call you Mister J?"

"Oh yes, doctor. I would like that very much."

"Okay, you don't like anyone in law enforcement, Mr. J."

"True." He said nonchalantly causing Harleen to unexpectedly crack up laughing, despite desperately trying to maintain a serious demeanor.

"I told you – laughs." He raised his hand to his mouth which had a tattoo of a laughing mouth on it.

She relaxed a bit and finally took a seat across from him on a bench in front of the table.

"Cute," she said "I like the tattoo."

"Thank you, Doctor. Now, I don't like what they're doing to you. A woman with your taste, strength and class shouldn't cave so easily – no matter what Redmond or your daddy happen to be holding over your head."

Her mind raced but she wanted to stay relaxed. "Thank you for the compliments. Interesting that you talk about my taste and strength, yet we've never met."

"Yes, but when a man finds out a beautiful woman is asking questions about them, well – I learned a few things too."

"Why did you really call me here?" She asked puzzled. "Was it to irritate my father or get under Thomas's skin because if so you failed. They're not going to know about our little session."

"No. I don't waste my time with them. I just wanted to see you, face-to-face, up close."

"Bull," Dr. Quinzel crossed her arms. "You never JUST want to see anyone and you hate psychiatrists and doctors. What's your game?"

"Why Dr. Quinzel, how much time have you dedicated into learning all about me? That a dangerous game, you're playing. Never-mind my reaction, what would daddy think?"

"Your reaction never crossed my mind and my father has nothing to do with this. Personally, I find atypical behavior interesting. That's why I became a psychiatrist and you are as atypical as they get."

"You flatter me,"

"I just mean I don't think anyone ever said you weren't fascinating. If we're being honest, you're the most fascinating man in Gotham, but that doesn't mean you are looking to be redeemed or truthfully seeking treatment."

"Most fascinating, man." He ignored the rest of what she said. "More fascinating than Batsy?"

"Bat-man? Is that what this is about? You want to know if I know something about the Batman. You think I know something because of my dad. I know the same thing you do. Batman is a narcissistic douchebag that my father, Thomas and Commissioner Gordon all have a hard-on for. He commits crime after crime and the city basically gives him a medal of honor for it. I know he's a grown man who wears tights, dresses like a Bat and talks in a deep silly voice. He probably belongs here more than you."

The Joker raised his head and laughed. "That does sum him up quite well. Oh Harley, you're never going to marry that bozo in blue."

"Really?" She asked with a bit of sarcasm, "by the way, my name is Dr. Harleen Quinzel. Not Harley. No one calls me Harley."

"Oh, I didn't tell you. Harleen Quinzel simply won't do. You don't want your father's last name anyways and you definitely don't want Tommy's. Harley Quinn is a much more suitable name. It gives you the gravitas you deserve."

A genuine sentimental smile emerged. "Like Harlequin? I get it. I like it." She relented and let her guard down even more.

"I knew you would. So, tell me, doll-face. How are you going to get out of marrying that imbecile?"

"I don't know. You wanna kill him for me?" They both laughed aloud.

"You would like that, wouldn't you? If I just broke out of here and shot Tommy boy right between the eyes."

"I was joking…"

"No you weren't. I know jokes. This was more wishful thinking. How about this – you get me out of here and I'll kill anyone you point at."

"Liar!" She laughed. "Even if I did want you to kill someone, the easiest thing for you to do, if I got you out of here, would be to kill me."

"Smart, too; and underneath that jacket of yours, I'd guess your figure isn't bad either."

She felt her face grow hot. "Thank you. I am very smart and my figure is good because of gymnastics. I was a gymnast in high-school and college, but, you'll have to trust me on that one. It'd be unprofessional for me to take my jacket off."

"Gymnastics, really, so you must be flexible in all the right ways." he smiled again and she found herself smiling back.

"I notice you aren't wearing the standard inmate jumpsuit," She needed to change gears.

"I'm not the standard inmate."

"There's no doubt about that." She said in a more flirtatious way than she meant. "but how did you get it?"

"They were all out of the orange so I had no choice but to bring in my own clothes. The cutbacks here are ridiculous. The last time the cafeteria served prime rib, it wasn't tender at all. I almost choked."

They both cracked up over his obvious lie. She took a deep breath determined to get back on track. "So can I assume you want me to be your doctor? I mean you wouldn't call me all this way and then send me packing, would you Mister J?"

"I'd never send you packing, Harley. Yes, be my doctor. Cure me. Fix all that's wrong. Where should we start? What deep dark secret do you want to know?" He gave her an evil gleam that made chills run down her spine.

"I think we - I think this was a good start and this is a good time to stop. Let's schedule another appointment." She took out her calendar and began looking through the dates."

"Leaving already. Has fear conquered you already?"

"NO! Not at all. I'm not afraid of you. It's just I have other appointments scheduled."

"Such dedication! I can't fault you for that. Alright, tomorrow. Come see me tomorrow morning, first thing."

"Tomorrow. Wow, you're just jumping in Mr. J. Okay, I'll move some stuff around. I'll be here at 7."

"Exactly 7. I detest tardiness."

"Exactly 7 it is. I'll have a few disclosures for you to sign. Nothing big. It's just the standard paperwork."

"I'll sign anything you want, but I can't sign in this thing."

She nodded at the straight jacket. "I'll get the guard to remove it for the paperwork."

"I would be eternally grateful if you would keep this silly thing off the whole session? It makes my arms so sore."

"Consider it done, but if you do anything or try anything...." She gave him a look of dominance.

"Oh, I wouldn't dream of it. Not with you, I like you."

"Good. Then we understand each other really well. I'll help you in any way I can and in turn, just don't kill me – or do, your choice really."

He started laughing aloud which caused her to crack up.

He rose from his seat, walked over to her, bent down kissed her hand. "I'll keep you around for now."

He then walked over to the exit and yelled for the guard who opened the door to lead him back to his cell.

A panicked thought entered Harley's head. She knew if Thomas or her father found out, she'd be reprimanded like a child and much more importantly, permanently taken off the case. 'I'll just have to make sure that doesn't happen,' she said to herself.

That night, Quinn was getting everything ready for her session with The Joker. She kept her door locked in the fear that her parents could enter at any time. She opted to use her personal computer since her father had full access to files at the asylum including who accessed them last. Her best chance of getting into The Joker's mind was to learn everything she could, without her father ever finding out.

That said, she needed to be prepared. Every other patient had been pushed out of her mind as Mister J consumed her every thought. She went through every piece of information she could find on the Clown Prince, growing more and more enthralled.

She looked at the Joker's arrests online and printed out some information. She found herself looking at pictures of The Joker more than reading the articles. He was splendidly mysterious and stood out regardless of how large the crowd was. In so many pictures, The Joker would be aside police officers or other criminals who were larger and physically stronger than him. Still, he was the main focus. Maybe it was charisma, dominance, depth, style–whatever it was, he stole the spotlight with ease.

The articles that she did read, she'd roll her eyes at. 'So bias. Of course, BATMAN is the hero. Gimme a break!'

After about a dozen that praised Batman, she grew so angry that she ended up commenting under her new alias, Harley Quinn.

"This is a disgrace! Where, may I ask, is the journalistic integrity? Batman is a violent, no-class vigilante who breaks the law. I can say from personal hands-on experience that when Mr. J was brought into Arkham, he was bloodied and bruised because Batman and the majority of Gotham PD has zero restraint. If Commissioner Gordon or Sgt. Quinzel had any balls at all, they'd be trying to arrest Batman instead of kissing his ass."

Moments after she posted her comment, her cell phone rang. At first, she sighed believing it to be Thomas, but the number however was blocked. She had a strange feeling that it may just be him.

"Hello,"

"Harley, so glad you took my call…"

"Mister J?" A thrill ran through her body. She spoke softly knowing her father was home. "I don't know whether to ask how you got my number or ask how you got to use the phone?"

"Let's not waste time. Don't ask either."

"Okay." She laughed. "What can I do for you?"

He let out a soft animalistic groan, "Oh, so many things, but most are difficult to do over the phone."

She couldn't find any words so after a few seconds of silence he continued. "I saw what you wrote under that libelous piece of trash parading itself as journalism. So many jump on the bandwagon to agree with whatever garbage the news regurgitates. It was refreshing to see someone so brave and articulate tell the truth."

"You saw the comment?" She was a bit flustered. "How did you know?"

"I know so many things."

"Yet reveal nothing. So, you hacked my computer." Surprisingly, even to herself, she wasn't angry.

"Guilty as charged." He said nonchalantly.

"That's definitely a talent. As for my comment, I just felt I had to say something because everyone is just so into this idiot in a bat suit."

"I agree. He's ridiculous and someone should take him down a peg or two."

"Most of Gotham needs to be taken down a peg or two. Not to change the subject, but did you call just because of what I wrote?"

"No."

"Then why"

"I was all alone, locked in my cell and thinking about all the fun we can have together. It became rather frustrating so I decided I wanted to have some fun now."

"I...I...I'm happy you did" she heard herself stammer, took a deep breath and then started again. "and I'm happy to help you in any way I can."

"I'm happy to hear that because there are so many ways you can help. Now, I don't want you to read too much about me. I want to surprise you." His voice was so demanding and filled with a dark lust that poured through the phone. Part of her wanted to focus on his treatment, but the other part of her just wanted to be near him.

"Then, we're on for 7 a.m."

"I live for it. By the way, Harley, have you broken things off with the bozo in blue yet?"

"Not yet…I mean, no. I haven't."

The Joker laughed which caused her to start laughing.

"You're very manipulative." She couldn't help smile. "You get me to say things, admit things that I don't intend to."

"It's another talent – one of many. Do me a favor, gorgeous."

"Yeah, I mean okay. I'm sorry, what's the favor, Mr. J?" She said as her face grew hot. She twirled her hair in her fingers and hung to his every word.

"When you come in tomorrow, don't wear some boring pantsuit underneath that god awful jacket. I want you to wear something special, something just for me."

"Mr. J…." That was too much. She couldn't go that far.

"Beneath that little white lab coat, put on something red and black and tight. You know, something that shows all those perfect little parts of you that you worked so hard to shape in gymnastics. It'll just be our little secret-something that tells me, I'm special."

"Mister J, I.... hello? Hello?" He hung up. She put the phone to her chest. "I'm not going to wear something just because he told me to." She rolled her eyes. "It would be completely unprofessional and send the wrong message." She walked over to her closet and just gazed at her wardrobe. "I can't believe he remembered everything I said. He's such a great listener – and killer. He's a killer. Okay, he may be a criminal but the man does know how to wear lipstick." The two voices in her head were combating each other. She looked down at her laptop where she had a pic of the Joker from an article she had pulled up, "and his hair is amazing. I mean, he knows style and if he thinks those colors will bring out my features….Goddammit!" She walked over to the closet and grabbed a red and black short tight dress she had never worn. She bought it at a midnight party that her friend was having. They sold lingerie, bras and sexy outfits. "Fuck it," she threw the dress on a chair and grabbed a red bra, matching panties and fishnets that she had purchased at the same party. "Hell, at least I'll get a chance to wear these." At that moment, the voice telling her to steer clear and stay professional died and never returned.

As she was getting everything ready, her phone rang again. This time she jumped to answer it, but paused as she saw the number. "Oh, hi Thomas….." she said softly.

"Were you expecting someone else?"

"No...no...what? Why would you ask that?"

"It's just the way you sound. Are you upset? Do you want me to come over?"

"Ummm...no." She rolled her eyes and thought 'I never want you to come over. You're a creep," but she knew she couldn't say that. "I am actually already in bed and mom fell asleep in the living room, I don't want her to wake up, not to mention I have to get up early. I'm seeing a patient tomorrow morning."

"Alright then. I do want to start planning the wedding though.'"

"I know you do. Bye." She hung up. Her phone rang again but seeing it was Thomas, she let it go to voicemail. She looked over at the dress. "Not to mention, I deserve a little excitement in my life."

Dr. Quinzel was behind the desk at 6:45. She quickly checked a small mirror. Her make-up was perfect. Her red lipstick popped with the dress. Her skin was smooth and she even put a bit of glitter on. It was the first time in a long time, she felt sexy.

The officer led The Joker in, but he was wearing the straight jacket. "

I said I needed his jacket off! I need Mister J to sign some documents."

"I don't think that's a good idea. He's really dangerous."

"If you're too afraid to do it, leave and I'll do it."

"Oh, you are a fun one, Harley." The Joker smiled at her.

"Dr. Quinzel, we don't want to get in trouble with the Sergeant. It's bad enough that you insisted we bring him to you and not saying anything."

"I'm his doctor. If you mention this to anyone including my father, I will make sure you are …."

"I know fired, fired. I got it, but I cannot remove the jacket. You want that done, you do it yourself." The guards walked out leaving the Joker smiling at her.

"Fucking cowards," she rolled her eyes.

"Harley, Harley, Harley, - look at you. You changed everything overnight." He said admiring her make-up. "I think I like when you do things for me."

She walked up to the Joker who looked her up and down.

"Who said I did it for you?" She untied the straight-jacket.

"And stockings." He let out a sound that could only be described as sexual. "They're fishnets. That's very promising." His tone was so dark it made her knees practically buckle.

"Well, sometimes I like dressing up." She looked into the Joker's eyes without a hint of fear. She walked in front of him and helped strip the jacket off. "There, that's better." He stood before her in a purple suit that fit him perfectly.

"Another purple suit. You must have so many connections."

She saw he wasn't responding so she dropped it.

"You look good in purple and green. It brings out your eyes and hair and complexion."

He leaned in. "Glad you noticed. Now, Let's see what the lovely doctor decided to wear." Before she knew what was going on, he had untied her white jacket and had it on the floor. "Oh, how I know you, Harley." He ran his hand down her side. "This is a great little number and it's new." She felt his fingers dance on her skin and let it happen. "I can tell."

"Ummm...yeah, well I bought it awhile back. I just never wore it."

"You never had a reason to. This is not a dress that Dr. Quinzel would wear, but for Harley Quinn, it's perfect."

"Thanks, thank you Mister J." She found herself lingering and taking in his compliment. Even when his hand fell behind her and to her rear, she said nothing.

"I need you..."

"You need me?"

Momentarily, she returned to planet earth, "I need you to sign that stuff." Her thoughts spun out of control, "please sit because we have work to do."

He ran his hand up and down a few more times and she naturally moved in the same direction of his hand. When he slid his fingers up her back, she would raise her chest out, and when he lowered them to her rear, she'd push against his hand.

After a few moments, he took a step back. "Okay, we'll do this your way, but only because you said please."

"What do you want to know?" He sat on the bench and it took her a moment to walk forward. She sat down and took a deep breath. She bit her bottom lip as her mind raced. The hundred questions she wanted to ask were at the tip of her tongue, but he was so wonderfully distracting. She couldn't take her eyes off of him and couldn't stop her body from reacting to him. He saw her lips trembling and watched her try to get herself together and fail.

"It's alright. I'll start" he was direct. "Do you have any ribbons in your bag?"

"Ribbons?"

"Hair ribbons. I want to see you put your hair up in ponytails - one on each side."

"I think so…" she said and without thinking tore through her purse and took out two hairbands. She pulled her hair to each side and put it up. "I actually love wearing my hair like this. This is the way I wear it when I go to bed."

"Tell me more." He said leaning in.

"There's nothing...nothing else to tell." She couldn't hide her stammering.

"I don't believe that for a minute. I want you to do me a favor,"

"Alright, what would you like me to do?" She asked in a tone that revealed she was all too willing.

"Where to start with that question…." He took a deep breath. "Your hair, wear it that way from now on: day, night, in bed, on the floor, on this table, standing, kneeling, anywhere you happen to be."

"Okay...Sure...I mean I'll do it." She said and took a deep breath, "Mister J, may I ask you something?"

"That's why we're here,"

"I know you despise psychiatrists and doctors. Why did you ask for me?"

"Harley, you know why. You're special to me."

"Because I wear what you tell me to?"

His teeth shined brightly as a Cheshire grin appeared on his face. "A lot of stupid people do what I say when I say, but you're not stupid. You're smart. You read my files. You hear all the horrible things that the doctors and newscasters have said, but can't seem to help yourself with me. That's definitely part of the attraction."

"You're attracted to me? You know, I like to form my own opinion about people." She knew that a line had now been crossed that could never be uncrossed. She felt herself growing excited and let her hand slowly fall to her leg and then up to her inner thigh. She moved against the seat, her body trying to satisfy the need her mind refused to acknowledge.

She saw him looking under the table and the urge to give him a show overpowered her. She widened her legs, lifted her dress and ran her finger against her panties.

His eyes were on her as a hungry sound escaped him. "As much as I love this sight, I can do better than that. Come over here. Now." He was demented and sick and wild and Harley dove in free-falling into his madness.

She rose from her bench and slowly, carefully, walked toward him fully aware that her red heels caught his eyes as they gleamed in the light.

She stopped aside him and stood waiting in anticipation of what he would do. He touched her leg and she couldn't help but lean in to him as he ran his hand up and down her thigh. Her fingers brushed through his hair.

"Gymnastics did you well,"

"Thank you,"

He stood up in front of her. He was silently daring her to make a move. His hand was wandering between her legs nearly at her center. She took a deep breath, moved forward and brushed her lips against his lightly. An electric shock ran through her body.

She went to kiss him again, but instead he took over. His mouth was on hers and his tongue demanded her lips part. He withdrew his hand from her thigh and placed it roughly on her rear and secured his other arm around her waist as he kissed her hard. She wrapped herself in his embrace and kissed him back letting her tongue wander his mouth.

He pulled away and straightened out his suit. She folded her hands in front of her. She knew he liked control and didn't mind giving into that.

"You wanna be my little sex kitten?" He said touching her mouth with his fingertip. She took his finger in her mouth. "Purr for me"

She rolled her tongue and made the noise he craved. He listened for a moment breathing heavily and then in an instant his mouth was on hers and his tongue owned her yet again.

He broke away. "Get on the table. Now, come on."

She stepped on the bench and then sat in front of him on the table. She was both flustered and excited. Her chest was moving up and down. The more she waited, the more lust filled her every cell. He kicked the bench across the room.

"the bozo in blue doesn't do it for you, does he Harley?"

"No, he doesn't." She said honestly. He roughly pushed her thighs open with his legs as he bent down and rested his arms on the table. He was only inches away from her sex and watched while his mere presence made her more and more aroused.

"He doesn't make you wet?"

"No. Never. Not even once. I don't want him. I don't want to think about him. I want you. I think about you. All last night, I couldn't stop. I couldn't stop touching myself."

"You should've come here. I would've taken a night visit."

"I should've." Her body was already reacting as she lifted herself up and down. Thomas wanted to come over and I couldn't. I couldn't see him."

"I know. I heard." He pulled her forward and kissed her hard again. "It's not your fault. How could you see him when you were thinking of me? The disappointment would've been endless."

"You tapped my phone. Clever." She said nonchalantly. He bit her ear as she groaned loudly. "hush now, you don't want the guards to rush in, do you?"

"No." she whispered "I want you. I need this more than anything. I've never – oh God, I've never wanted anyone like this before."

"Then take off that ring." He turned serious and dark. The mere glimpse of her promise to another made him a little red.

"Here, take it." She took if off and put it in his palm.

He put the ring in his pocket and then raked his hands over her breasts, satisfied with her loyalty. His fingers quickly drifted down to her legs. "The reason I love fishnets," he said as he pulled them apart, "is they're so easy to tear."

"M-i-s-t-e-r J, you are fire." She said almost in a trance. She raised her waist begging him to touch her.

"And you're the girl sticking her hand in the flame. You know, Harley," He spoke as he licked and bit her inner thigh. "I could do anything right now. I could kill you." Lick. "I could fuck you and then kill you." Bite. "Hell, I could kill you and then fuck you." Harder bite. He broke the skin but she didn't care.

"I have a request, Mister J."

"Yeah…" he said and then ran his finger against her panties. "so wet for me. Such a naughty girl. I'm sorry what was your request"

"Oh fuck, If you are going to kill me, just please please fuck me, first."

He began laughing. "You did ask nicely," he pushed her down on the table and climbed on top of her. He was so hard against her. "I can feel you. Oh, that is all you." She wrapped one leg around him to feel him even closer. He pushed her dress down exposing her red bra.

"Haven't been with a real man in a while, huh Harley?"

"Judging by you I'd say this is the first time." She began circling herself around his hardness. "I want to be yours. Own me."

"I already do." His body was piercing hers. The sensation was driving her wild. The Joker watched as Harley's body desperately tried to fuck him through his clothing. "Good girl, that's it, take what you want." he said and moved her head up to bite her neck.

He ripped off her bra and his mouth was immediately on her breasts. He would gently lick her and then bite until he tasted blood. His fingers ran down her side and then up her thigh until it reached the center.

"Oh God Mister J."

"I don't know about you Kitten, but God has nothing to do with me. I just know where to touch you. I know how to touch you." He flicked her warmth causing an even more intense need in her. He saw her flinch as she moaned once more.

"I want to feel you. I want to feel you inside of me."

"Beg me. Say it." She began to gyrate on his hand. He pulled it away and when she went to lower her own hand, he pinned both of hers down. "I said beg me, Harley. Say what you want. Let me hear you beg me to fuck you."

She pushed her head hard against the table. "Please fuck me. I'll do whatever you want. I just need it." She was trembling while saying it unable to stop her body from moving against nothing.

He unzipped his pants, took himself out, pushed her panties aside and without warning entered her hard. She couldn't help but yell out in pleasured pain. It was as if his body was made to be in hers. He was Adam and she Eve. Her climax washed over her. She rocked against him matching each of his hard strokes and grunts. "There, oh there, there," she came again and again against him. When he felt her body twitching, he pushed harder making her feel his full length.

She moved her body in a circular motion to get him to the edge. "I want to feel you come inside of me."

"You want that." He said still thrusting.

"Yes, yes. Please"

"That is the magic word." He pinned her hands up behind her, grunted hard and spilled his seed in her.

He rolled off of her, stood up as her body still moved. He buckled his pants and straightened his suit. She remained for a few moments leaving her bare breasts fully exposed and letting her fingers dance on her twitching sex.

"Harley," The Joker's tone became demanding and it woke her from her orgasmic heaven.

She sat up still out of breath, pulled up her dress and nodded. "Yeah, puddin…."

"Break up with Thomas, tonight. I don't care what you tell him, but if he touches you" he laughed a bit and then grabbed a-hold of her chin roughly. "he'd be touching something that's mine – and I can't have that."

She nodded quickly. "I'll call him now if you want. I'll do whatever you want."

"I want." He said in a serious enough tone that she jumped off the table, fixed her dress and retrieved her cell. She put Thomas on speakerphone.

"Harleen, I'm glad you called. We need to get this wedding together."

"It's Harley," Harley smiled at The Joker who moved his fingers forward as if to tell her to keep talking. "It's Harley Quinn now. I changed my name and I changed some other stuff. Listen, I don't want to marry you. I don't love you. I really can't stand you. My dad was harassing my mom about the whole damn thing and you were a dick and encouraged him to do it until I said 'yeah' but I don't want to marry you and I'm not going to."

"What? Harleen? What's going on? I don't know what you're talking about, but I'm coming over right now…"

"Oh but now's not a good time," The Joker grabbed the phone and began pacing wearing the confidence of a man who owned the world. "Tommy boy, Joker here. You really need to take a hint. You see, Harley is a bit out of it because I just fucked her on the visiting table here at Arkham and she is a tired little thing after what she's been through. Isn't that right, Harley?"

"Yes. I can still feel you." She rubbed her genuinely sore legs.

"Poor Harley. I can't even imagine what her insides are going through. Harley, baby, lift your dress for me. Show me your wetness." She did as she was told and stood before him fully exposed. "Good girl. Yeah, Redmond. I can see why you'd want her, but there's no way you could handle Miss Quinn. She needs a real man who knows more than missionary position and you don't fit the bill. Say goodbye, pumpkin…"

"Bye Tommy…wish I could say it was fun."

The Joker hung up on Thomas and looked at Harley. She went to lower her skirt, but he raised his hand.

"Give me a moment. Touch yourself."

She began rubbing herself in front of him. She lifted one leg and extended it on the table to give him a better show.

"You are something amazing, Mister J." She said as she penetrated herself. "Uh-huh, yes, yes," she whispered until she shuddered coming again. "The things you do to me."

"and this is just the intro." He walked over to her and lowered her dress to its normal position. She withdrew her hand.

"I never felt like this."

"You want more?" He kissed her lips hotly. "How much more of me do you want?" He asked looking her dead in the eyes.

"I want all of you" She said without hesitation.

"Tommy, your father and all of Gotham PD will be here in the next ten minutes. If you want me, you gotta get me out of here."

It didn't take a second for her to think of a plan. "Hold me hostage," She put her white jacket on and tied it trying to look as kept as possible. She then grabbed a knife from her purse and handed it to him.

"You are a brave girl," He opened it, brought it to her neck and purposely pinched it a bit causing it to bleed. He licked it away. "This should be fun." He smiled.

"Showtime, puddin." She said, kissed him hard and then screamed for what sounded like dear life. The guards came barreling in, machine guns drawn.

"Don't do anything stupid!" The Joker warned. "I will slice and dice this sexy little kitten into 1000 pieces and who here wants to explain that to her daddy?"

The guards backed up. "I told you not to take off the jacket!"

"I'm sorry!" Harley yelled in mock fear. "I thought it would be fine."

"Okay. Listen Whatever you want? Just let Dr. Quinzel go."

"This sounds like, Let's make a deal. One of my favorite game shows. Okay, let's make a deal. You give me your guns and I'll let the doc go." The guards looked at each other and tightened their grip on their weapons.

"DO IT!" Harley yelled. "If I die, my father will kill you both."

They reluctantly put the guns down and their hands up.

"Good job, men." The Joker told them and then released his grip on Harley. "You're free to do whatever you want."

Harley quickly lunged and had both guns in her hand before the guards knew what was happening. She tossed one to The Joker. "Gymnastics." She said with a smile.

The Joker shot both men in the head and took a deep breath. "I love the smell of gun powder."

Harley saw a cop down the hall, from the corner of her eye. He was trying to hide. "Hold on, puddin. We got a sneak. I don't like sneaks." She shot the officer dead and then nodded. "Okay, now, we're clear."

"And you're a good shot!" He smiled and hit her on the rear. "Let's get out of here. I want to get you home. I have so many toys to show you."

"I don't know if I should be scared or turned on," she said following him.

"Both," He replied with all the seriousness in the world.

They got to the parking lot and she led him to her red convertible corvette. "Give me the keys."

"Why do you get to drive?" She asked handing them to him and getting in the passenger side.

"Because you're going to be too busy putting me in that beautiful little mouth of yours." He said starting the car, pulling her near on top of him and racing out of the parking lot. "You know how long I've been wanting to fuck you?"

"How long?" She asked feeling herself grow more excited.

"Come here and find out. Give daddy what he likes."

"This is the biggest rush I've ever had and you, YOU are the sexiest man in the world." She confessed and then licked his neck.

"Put those lips to good use and show me how sexy I am," he said driving 90 miles an hour with one hand on the wheel and using his other to push Harley's head downward.

She let out a giggle and unzipped his pants letting out his fully erect cock. "You are amazing," She admired the length and width for a moment and then touched him lightly.

"Don't play with me, kitten. I don't like gentle and I hate slow." He said breathing deep.

She lowered her mouth and began licking and sucking the shaft.

"That's it. That's my girl." He shoved himself upward urging her to take him in wholly. The gas pedal was to the ground.

She tasted every part and reveled when he let out approving guttural groans. She was taking him fully in her mouth, when the car abruptly stopped. She would've fallen forwards had he not held her still. She brought her head up and looked around and noticed she was in a garage. "Are we home?"

"keep going."

He pushed her head down hard and she lowered her mouth back onto him. He started thrusting faster and faster fucking her mouth. His breaths became short and she could feel him nearly there. She wrapped her tongue around his shaft and rolled her hand against him moving up and down quickly.

He came in her mouth and held her until while she swallowed and licked him clean.

She flung back against the passenger side and rested her arm on him, while he put himself back in his pants.

"Yeah, we're home, come on." He got out of the car and held the door for her. She got out quickly and followed him inside the dark home. "Oh I love this." The purple and green color scheme was gorgeous. "I love this."

"Good. He took a shot of whiskey from the small bar he had in the living room and gave her a shot which she swallowed just as quick. She then licked her lips.

"Let's get you to the bedroom." He lifted her an inch or so off the ground and he had her dress off before she even realized it was gone.

He tossed her on the bed.

"Mister J, today was the most fun I have had my whole life. It's like there was a part of me missing."

He laid down on the bed and pulled her on top of him. He pushed his cock against her hard. He was already fully erect and ready to go. "And I filled it?"

"Yeah you did," She said and then began moving against him. She withdrew him from his pants once again and then took off her panties. She lowered herself on him. The sensation of him entering made her moan loudly. She began grinding her hips against him and tightening herself on him. "You're like a machine."

"Too much for you?" He asked. "I'd been in that nuthouse for almost a year. So, daddy's ready to play. Can you keep up?"

"Oh yeah, I can keep up."

"Good girl - back there, killing that cop without a thought. That was good." He let out a grunt as he thrust up. "And already being up for round two despite our little workout. I like that too."

"My body is ALWAYS ready for you." She moved her waist up and down quickly. He groaned again as she went back and forth, and up and down. "and I'm flexible," she bragged.

The Joker opened his eyes and pulled her hair hard. "What would you do for me, huh?" He said staring at her.

"Anything. Name it. Die for you. Kill for you. " Her body was already on the brink.

He jerked his hips up hard.

"You're my prize….my toy….you're JUST for me."

His words sent her over the edge. "Only for you, Mister J. Just you."

"You say the right things." He flipped her over and begin fucking her fast. "How's that feel?"

"Harder...harder...harder...More…." She wanted him to know she could take him, anywhere, anytime. She could handle it.

He held on to the headboard and forced himself into her so hard that her head flung backward. "You like that?" He asked unrelenting.

"More," she demanded, pushing back and meeting every thrust. "You're a fucking God," Her nails dug deeply into his skin. The deeper she dug her nails, the harder he fucked her.

She was hit hard and came again. Her moan echoed through the house. He grunted one last long time and let his climax spill over her. His tongue traveled from her waist to her neck as her body continued to spasm.

She tried to catch her breath. "It's this part. Right now. It's like an after-shock." She said taking his hand and resting it on her wet sex. ". You make me alive." She sat up and kissed him hard. "I need a cigarette. Haven't had one since I was 16, but I need one."

He went into the drawer by the bed, pulled a lighter and cigarette out and lit it. He took a long drag and then handed it to her. She sat up on her elbows took it in and handed it back.

"We gotta get some serious cash. Money is power. The Gotham PD froze my accounts when they threw me in the pen."

"Assholes," she said shaking her head but he noticed she wore a victorious smile.

"Are you in the afterglow, my dear or do you have an Ace up your sleeve." He took one last puff and put it out.

"I don't know. Do you consider 3.5 million or so, an Ace?"

The Joker turned to her and smiled sensing she was serious. "Where, when and how, doll-face?"

"Not so fast," she waved her finger. "If I tell you, you gotta grant me a wish."

He got on top of her and pushed her down hard. "Harley, don't mess around with me." He rested his arm on her neck forcefully, but not enough to cut off the air.

"I'm not. I wouldn't. I swear. You'll get every dime."

He relaxed his hold and his demeanor lightened as quickly as it had grown dark. "Okay, kitten what's your wish?"

"I want to be like you…" she touched his face.

"Be like me?"

"Yeah, I mean your skin, your lips, your hair – I know there's some chemical that does this. I want it. I don't want to be made in anyone's image but yours. Make me in your image."

He nodded and slowly got off of her. "I can arrange that." He took her hand and ran it over his neck. "You want to be like this…"

"Yes, I want to feel your skin on my face and on my body." She closed her eyes getting aroused at the thought of it.

"It's very painful."

"I want the pain. Every moment of it. Please."

He licked his lips. "I knew you were something special," he brought her fingers to his lips and grazed each one with his teeth. "And the cash?"

"Right," she smiled and opened her eyes. "My father, the honorable sergeant, has been bribed, stole from the evidence room, lied about how much money he found during stakes, he's a complete scumbag. He has a safe in his office and I know his password."

"And there's 3.5 million in there…"

"At least. Probably, more like 4…"

He let out a near orgasmic grunt. "Good girl."

"Just one more thing…" she held her finger up. "You can kill my father-you can do whatever you want to that hypocrite asshole. If Tommy is there, we can shoot him, stab him, whatever. I don't care about him at all. My mom is the only one

… You gotta leave her out of it. I mean, if we gotta tie her up, that's fine, but my mom's been hurt enough for 2 lifetimes. She's a doormat who tried her best and she's not like the rest of the world. My dad and sis tried to lock her up in Arkham and I wouldn't let them. Oh and speaking of my sis, she's uptight as hell. Her name is Pam and she's married to Officer Pollock..."

"James Pollock - I hate that guy."

"Me too. He's a douchebag. They'll probably be there waiting for me to return, apologize and agree to marry Tommy so we may have to improvise with them, but as long as my mom makes it out – I don't care."

"Mommy will survive. You have my word..."

"I knew you'd understand. Thanks. I kind of wanted to go by home to pick up some of my stuff anyways so this works out." She hugged The Joker. "We gotta be careful with my dad. He has 3 cellphones. His work, his regular and the one for his whores – we have a house phone, and he has 4 guns in the house. He always has one on him."

"I'm not worried." He said looking at her. He touched her face. "Sgt. Daddy, other than having whores, what else did he do?"

"What didn't he do." Harley sort of laughed as she fought back tears. "The latest was this" she moved her hair away from her shoulder and showed a deep wound that was turning into a scar. "This was for me saying I wasn't marrying Tommy at that god awful engagement party. Half of Gotham was there. Tommy stood there looking at the floor and at the ceiling and everywhere other than a my father beating me. Prick. I held my ground and still said no, but then Daddy Dearest decided to hurt me the one way he knew he could. He said he'd send my mom to Arkham if I didn't agree. She's not well, but she doesn't need to be in a hospital. I hate this fucking town. Everybody heard him say this shit and no one did anything. What could I do?"

"Kill them all."

"Yeah," she nodded getting revved. "That's what I want."

"Why did daddy Sgt. want you to marry Redmond?"

"Power. Tommy keeps quiet about all of my dad's bullshit. Tommy and James kissed my father's ass, gave him money. So many cops did that and the single ones like Tommy did it even more. Me and my sis basically bought me off an auction. The only difference is I didn't want to be put up for sale."

The Joker kissed the wound and let out a laugh. "Well, it'll be fun to see how much daddy Sgt. likes power when his insides are on his outsides. First things first, let's grant your wish before we hit the road. Let's show the family that Doctor Harleen Quinzel is officially dead."

"Long live Harley Quinn!" She smiled.

The Joker brought her into the basement and as he went down the stairs he gently took her hand and guided her down. He was rough and demented and dark, but there was also an old-fashioned classy romantic style he displayed. She loved it all.

Once downstairs, The Joker turned on the light and revealed a large vat of bubbling liquid. On the side it said "ACE CHEMICALS,"

"Home delivered?"

"When they remodeled a few years ago, I borrowed some."

She walked over eagerly. "Then, this really is the stuff?" she went to put her hand in but he stopped her.

"Careful. Once this is done, there's no going back."

"I don't want to go back. I just want to go forward"

A groan of pleasure escaped his lips. "You'll belong to me. Every part of you."

"I already do. Don't you know, Mister J, you own my soul."

"The Joker stared at her and smiled. He pointed to the ladder and she walked up. At the top step, he started counting.

"1, 2…"

"3" She said and then dove in as if it were a swimming pool.

He watched her become engulfed in the bubbles. All the pigment from her skin began disintegrating in the liquid. Her skin, just moments ago dark and tanned was now white as blow. 'Beautiful' He was mesmerized by the sight.

Harley's blonde hair now had bright red strands mixed it on one side and bright dark blue strands mixed in on the other. Her loyalty, her willingness to surrender, to fight the world but to give in to him – it was a powerful aphrodisiac. He never wanted a woman more.

He jumped in after a few moments brought her to the surface and placed her gently on a makeshift deck and shower he had next to the vat.

She was still unconscious when he put on the water. He made sure it was warm and then washed her and himself off. She slowly came to and noticed her hand right away. If she felt pain, she didn't show it.

"It worked! Puddin, you did it." She touched her own skin. "You did this. You're a God and this basement is like Eden."

He shut the water off, walked up to her and pulled her close. "I'm YOUR God. That's all that matters. Now, let's go get our money." He kissed her hard and she kissed him just as hard backing him against the wall. Energy surged through her.

"Everything you are is on me, inside of me. I can feel you. You made me." She was still gleaming and glowing in her own skin. "I want to rule the world with you."

"We go to the house. Kill a bunch of people. Bring the money back here and then I promise I will bring you to the darkest most depraved place you could ever dream of." He laughed hauntingly.

"I can't wait"

Upstairs, he rounded up a group of men and gave them orders. Meanwhile, Harley was getting dressed. She put her panties and torn fishnets back on, she had a pair of red and blue shorts in her bag and a plain white shirt with a red collar that stretched to the shoulders. "Too plain," she thought and then noticed a gold marker on the desk and grabbed it. "Property of Joker" she wrote on it and then threw it on. As she stepped out of the room, she heard The Joker say, "No one hurts mother. She's off limits. We get there, and you two bring the mother in the back bedroom."

"I thought no one was off limits. You getting soft cuz of this chick?" One of the guys said with a laugh.

The Joker laughed. "Good one. That's a good one." The man stopped laughing and stammered out an apology. It wasn't enough as The Joker shot him in the chest. "Anyone else want to share commentary about Harley. I am open to any suggestions."

Harley broke out laughing, "Bang Bang, he's dead." She called over as The Joker turned around. Not taking his eyes off of her he yelled to them, "Get rid of the body and be in the van in 3 minutes."

The Joker led her out and into the back of a large white van.

"You see what I wrote on my shirt…" She pushed out her chest proudly.

"I like that. I'll put it on you permanently when we get back. You sure you know the password."

"yep, it's 09131992Alicia… It's the most recent whore's birthday and her name. Yeah, he's a class act." She grabbed a gun from the floor and loaded it.

"1992, So he went young…"

"Yep, same age as me…actually 8 months younger than me. We were in the same class. She was a friend." She grew angrier as she spoke.

"Look at me, Harley."

Harley knelt in front of him as if he were the messiah and she his disciple.

"It's just me and you. These guys, are dispensable. I can go down to Main Street or Wayne Blvd and pick up 1000 other just like them. You and me though, we're the same now – same species – same organism – same skin. I need you to be strong for me? No going back, you understand right?"

"YES." She said with a definitive answer. "Everything you've ever said is right. Life really IS just one big joke. I'm just not going to be the punchline anymore."

The Joker nodded and then kissed her hotly as the men loaded in the van. He broke away. "Drive," he ordered.

They arrived at the house and the men surrounded it as the Joker helped Harley from the van.

Four of the men entered the back entrance and two entered with The Joker and Harley.

Chaos ensued as the men ordered the whole family to sit down. They patted Sgt Quinzel down.

"Get his cell phones and all his guns. He definitely has one on his right side." Harley ordered and then turned softly to her mother. "Mom, don't freak out. You're going to walk with these two gentlemen and they're going to put you in the back bedroom. They're not gonna hurt you, but you just gotta listen to them. We're here cuz I just need to pick up a few things." She looked at the men who began walking with her mom. "If you hurt her, I will cut your dicks off and feed them to Mister J's hyenas."

"I'd listen to her. Bud and Lou do have very odd tastes." The Joker warned with a glare.

They nodded and walked her mother down the hall.

"Harleen? What the hell is going on?" the Sergeant said looking over his daughter.

"It's Harley, now. Harley Quinn. I gave up your last name because you're a bad person and Mister J came up with a much better - much more fitting name." She caught eye of her sister who was being tied up. "Oh puddin, that's my sister Pam, the uptight one I told you about. Pam meet the Clown Prince of Gotham, Mr. J" She was smiling proudly when she said it. "and of course douchebag James is here." She sighed and turned to the men. "James is a cop so check him and check Tommy really good too. They get trained to be sneaky. I hate sneaks. I hate cops."

"Me too." The Joker smiled menacingly when he saw Thomas. "And, here he is - in the flesh - Thomas Redmond. We talked earlier. I'm sorry, we had to let you go so quickly." The men tied Tommy up as The Joker motioned for Harley. "Crawl to me, kitten."

She seductively got on all fours and crawled to him. Once she reached him she purred like a kitten.

He reached out his hand and helped her stand. He walked behind her and wrapped his arms tightly around her waist. He pulled her close, so that she stood directly in front of her ex.

"Tell little Tommy what we did today." He kissed her neck.

"My God, Harleen, you're all white. What the hell did he do to you? That's my fiancé. Get your hands off of her."

"He did everything to me – over and over and over again." Harley didn't care if she was alone or if everyone in the country was in the room. When the Joker was near her, she wanted him.

"It had just been so long since Harley had a good time, and she had an itch that she begged me to scratch." The Joker began rubbing her breasts with one hand and her upper thigh with the other. "She's so insatiable." The Joker moved his hand from her leg to her center.

She instinctively fell onto him and widened her legs. She closed her eyes and moved her body against him.

The Joker took the ring Tommy had given Harley out of his pocket. "Nice rock." The Joker ran it over Harley's breast. "I know you wanted it to bring my sex toy some good times. Since you're not UP to the task, I'll take care of it." Brazenly, he rubbed the diamond against Harley's nipple until it grew so hard it could be seen through the shirt.

"You know every place…" she mumbled through small moans of ecstasy.

"What about this place?" He whispered in her ear as he brought the ring down to her sex. She rocked against it and lowered her hand to hold his still. The Joker could feel her wetness on his fingers.

He laughed knowing she couldn't resist him even then. "Right here, baby, come for me. Show Tommy what a real man can do for you."

Her body tightened as her clit began pulsating. She closed her legs on his arm and moved up and down. Everything disappeared as she was rocked to the core. "There, and there, Yes, Oh God, Mister J." Her nails dug into The Joker's hand.

"HARLEEN! Wake up! What the hell are you doing and what happened to you? What did this maniac do to you?"

She didn't respond. She took a few deep breaths and then opened her legs enough to let the Joker's arm free.

"Purr for me, kitten." He devilishly said as he ran her own wetness against her lips.

She did so for him until he stopped her with a kiss. "Go get the cash. I'll be there in a few." He hit her rear and watched her walk down the hall. "She is something special, isn't she Tommy?"

"What did you do to her?"

"I created her. I'm Frankenstein and she's my monster."

"You brainwashed her!"

"Whatever I did, she's my little sex kitten now – does whatever I say." He eyed Tommy, "I can see that you still want her." The Joker spotted a bright gold gaudy Cross on his neck. "and you're a Christian."

"Yes, Yes I am. Are you?"

"No, but that doesn't matter. You are; and The Bible says, if your eye causes you to sin, gouge it out. You gotta follow the rules" He took a knife from his pocket and stuck it deeply into Tommy's left eye. Tommy screamed in pain and the Joker just laughed. "It isn't nice to look at another man's woman especially when that man is me."

The Joker looked around the room and smiled the most genuine smile he had in years. "I'm going to have so much fun with you and the good ole Sgt." He then turned his attention to his men. "Keep them tied up and watch them. Especially, Tommy boy and the Sgt. Any trouble, kill them."

He walked over to Harley who was down the hall. "Over here," She called from her father's office. The Joker walked in and was shocked to see, Harley was already loading the cash from the safe.

"Look at you, baby." He smelled the money and ran a stack through his fingers. "You did real good."

"Thank you." She gave him a smile, "I heard Tommy yelling. What'd ya do?"

"Nothing big. Not yet. So, what are we looking at – dollar figure?"

"I got it all but that one last pack down there. It's another 10 grand bringing us up to nearly 5 million dollars."

"That's my girl."

"Could you give me a lift so I can get that last stack." She was a little seductive in her tone and played with the bottom of her shirt a bit showing off her slim, bright white stomach.

He walked over and wrapped his arm tightly around her and lifted her placing his fingers right against her shorts. He put her up against the wall and nearly into the safe while he penetrated her.

"My insatiable little kitten, are you playing a game? I know you could've gotten that all by yourself."

He started pushing in her harder.

She began riding him quickly. "YES… YES….."

Her climax washed over her entire body. She grabbed the safe as her body shook. He then put her on the ground and held her still as she nearly lost her balance.

"All wet. Bad girl," He said in mock disapproval as he placed his fingers in front of her. "Taste it,".

She sucked on his fingers. "That's all your doing, but it tastes good." She said with a smirk. She easily pulled herself back up to the safe and grabbed the last stack. "You were right. That was easy." She smiled at him. "Here's your money, Mister J." She handed him the bag.

He fanned some of the stacks. "Where can we go in this house to really celebrate."

"I gotta run to my bedroom and grab some clothes and stuff - change out of my panties."

"Your bedroom. Yes, let's go grab some things out of your bedroom."

She led him to the first door on the left and opened it. The décor was bright pink. She had a twin size bed. He sat down. "This is a horrible room. It's too bright and dull. No wonder you went crazy and ran off to my circus."

She started laughing.

"You, Harley, get the joke. I may just keep you. Show me what you want to take."

She looked at her clothing and grabbed some other items she had bought from her friend's party. Tight leather and lace lingerie and clothing. She grabbed some high heeled white and black boots and put them next to him.

She went into her drawer and grabbed her sexy panties and bras that hadn't been worn.

"These are fun and all brand new."

"I never had a reason to wear them before."

"Really - never?"

"Never. No one ever knew the buttons to push with me." She took off her shirt revealing her breasts and then slipped out of her shorts. The Joker leaned back on the bed and watched.

"You on the other hand….do things to me." She let her palm run down her neck to her breast it moved downward and underneath her panties to her center. "Just thinking about you makes me come." Her hips buckled a bit at she began stroking herself faster.

"That's it Harley, bring yourself there."

She opened her legs and began a circling motion with her hips. Her head fell back "OH, Mister J."

He pulled her to him and pushed her on the bed. He knelt in front of her. "Keep touching yourself." He ordered as he slid off her shoes, fishnets and panties. He started leaving small bites on her leg and inner thigh. He watched as her movements on her hand became quicker. He forcefully took her hand in his and harshly touched the spot he knew would get her. "It's right here" he said into her ear.

"OH FUCK!" she cried out to his delight. He already had his cock out and was pressing it against her.

"Say you want it." He said roughly in her ear. "Loud enough for everyone to hear."

She stared him dead in the eye and yelled out. "Fuck me, Mr. J! Fuck me. I want it! I want it! I'll do whatever you want just please." She was pushing against his cock, her body pleading for him to enter. With full force he obliged. He pulled her hair hard and stuck his tongue in her mouth. She jerked her hips up to him.

"That's it. Fuck me back. Fuck me back." He let out a few small grunts. "Purr…show me you're a good little sex kitten, purr, for daddy."

She purred until he hit the right spot again. "OH, I'm there, Mister J. I'm there.. I'm here. Don't stop. Don't stop." Words changed to sounds of pleasure. He came hard and groaned.

After a few moments, he got dressed and helped her up. He threw her clothes in a bag as she slipped on her shirt and a new pair of panties and shorts. "You are incredible." She kissed him again.

"Yes, I am. Let's go torture the Sgt. and show the family who you belong to. Unless, you changed your mind."

She leaned in and kissed him hard, her body shuddered. She licked her lips and danced her fingers against her sex. "I haven't changed my mind about anything." She purred once more making him smile.

"Then let's have some fun."

She giggled as he opened the door and walked out before her.

"So, anything happen while we were gone?" The Joker looked around.

Harley noticed Tommy's eye right away. She giggled and pointed causing the Joker to smile.

"Gimme a break. That's why he was yelling?" She shook her head.

"Yeah, apparently no appreciation for pain. He should've told me before I took his eye."

Harley burst out laughing. "Good one, Mr. J.

She then saw her sister staring at her with a disgusted look.

"Oh go to hell, Pam. You can think whatever you want. I gave up caring."

"Clearly! You have to stop this. You obviously need some help. You have something seriously wrong with your head. You always have."

The Joker walked up to Pam and struck her hard in the face with the barrel of his gun. "That wasn't a nice thing to say to your sister. Apologize."

Harley smiled and found herself to be standing taller. "Thank you, puddin." Pam's husband struggled to get up. The Joker cocked the pistol and shot him in the knee.

"I'll have to ask you to please remain in your seat."

Harley clapped in glee. "My guy is sexier than your guy, tougher than your guy and just shot your guy." She gushed.

The Joker turned to Pam and hit her again. "I said apologize to Harley."

"Leave her alone!" Sgt. Quinzel yelled over. "Get away from her and leave now! You want to take Harley, take her I don't care."

"As if you ever did." Harley chimed in.

"Come now, Sgt. It's Pam's turn now." The Joker moved closer to Pam. "Apologize to Harley"

Harley folded her arms. "I'm waiting."

"Leave me alone. Let dad go. Untie all of us and just leave."

The Joker rolled his head around and let out an annoyed grunt. "This is really easy. Pam, that's your name, right. It's fitting. It's an average name for an average girl. So Pam" The Joker knelt beside her and took out the knife he used to gouge Tommy's eye out. He placed it against Pam's mouth. "If you don't sincerely apologize to your sister, you won't ever be able to say another word again."

Harley blew a kiss to The Joker and then happily said, "So, Pam, is it an apology or snip-snip no more tongue?"

Realizing there was no way to reason, Pam nodded. "I'm sorry Harleen…" she slipped up and saw that the Joker was already pulling on her chin. "Harley. I'm sorry Harley. I was out of line. I'm just really scared, but I'm sorry."

"I, as the bigger person, accept your apology." Harley smiled.

"say 'thank you'" he ordered Pam.

"Thank you," she said with grit teeth.

"That was the first time she ever said sorry." Harley walked over smiling. "Even if you had to threaten to take her tongue out, it's an improvement. I should've done that years ago."

The Joker and Harley both laughed prompting the Joker's crew to laugh along. "Now, Let the games begin." He announced.

"Since, the Sgt was so keen on interrupting. We'll start with him. What's your plan?"

Harley looked at her father. Every bad thing he ever did went through her mind. she turned back to the Joker. "Mister J, I want to kill him. After everything he did to my mom and me. I want to."

"Wow. I'm impressed. You want to be the one to actually put his lights out for good?" He asked as he placed both arms on her shoulder.

"Yes,"

The Joker reveled in the thought. "Ask me."

"Please. Please let me do it."

"How could I say 'no' to that face." he went to hand her the gun.

"Too easy for him." She grabbed a knife from the bag of money. "I want to use this."

"Oh, I like that." The Joker stepped out of the way and outstretched his arm to guide her directly to him.

Everyone began yelling, but neither Harley nor the Joker heard. Their focus was on the Sgt.

Harley turned to her father. "Dad do you recognize your hunting knife?" She leaned down and showed a scar down her right arm. "This is from our camping trip I was 7. I saw a deer eating grass and I pretended to be a dear and ate grass too. You said, if I acted like an animal you were gonna treat me like an animal. Well, dad you made me an animal and I've just been released from my cage. Mister J gave me the key."

Harley took the tape off her father's mouth. "Any last words?"

"For God sakes Harleen, I don't remember that at all. If I did do something like that it was to teach you right from wrong. You were wild and needed guidance."

"I needed love!" she yelled back. "You never care about me or mom. You only gave a damn about Pam because she jumped when you said how high, but all of that is over. You're going to get every ounce of pain you caused returned to you right now."

The Joker lightly leaned against Harley to get a view of the action. He grew anxious and aroused. His maniacal laughter drowned out the protests. "I have to see this. Guys keep the guns on the rest of the bunch. Harley, do it, do it baby. Make me proud."

"Harleen! Put that down. What are you thinking? What is wrong with you?" The Sgt pleaded.

"Come on," The Joker pushed himself into her backside. The gleam from the knife turned him on. "Do it, baby. Stab him. For everything he did to you and everything he did to your mom. Teach him a lesson."

"Don't listen to that freak! He's using you. Harleen, come on. I'll do better."

Harley took the knife and jabbed it deep in her father's stomach. "The name is Harley Quinn!" She kept stabbing him over and over again as she continued to yell. "Why is that so hard to remember? You remember every name of every whore you've ever been with. And Mister J, is not a freak. He's a fucking God!"

The Joker watched on gleefully fascinated with her intensity. He finally put his hand on her shoulder. "Here. Watch this!" he took the knife jabbed it into one lung, turned and then did the same to the other lung. He withdrew the weapon and handed it to Harley.

The Sargent's yells and protests became weaker and more confused.

"That was amazing, pumpkin. And now for the show." He pulled Harley close. She could feel him rock hard against her. Instinctively, she pushed back on his cock. He wrapped his arms around her and ran his hands underneath her shirt.

"Watch him bleed out. Look at the pain in his eyes. You did that. His whole pathetic life is just draining out of him." He kept his eyes on the Sgt but lowered his lips to Harley's neck and ran his hands down her waist letting his fingers dance between her legs.' "He's almost gone. Say goodbye,"

"Bye." She whispered already in a trance of ecstasy.

The Joker let out a near orgasmic sigh. "You did great. I knew red was your color." He whispered in her ear. "a beauty basking in the blood of her father – it's poetry. If there wasn't any work left, you'd be on the floor right now."

Harley turned to him and kissed him hard. She grabbed a pillow and lowered herself to all fours. Kneeling in front of him she spoke soft and seductively, "I can still be on the floor. If you want me here." Towering over her, he had a perfect viewing of her size D cleavage from her V neck shirt.

Pam started crying hysterically, "Get up! What is wrong with you? The guy is a fucking maniac. You just killed dad!"

Harley turned her head to her sister, but The Joker turned her face back to him. "Forget about her. She can wait. Let her wait. Let's do this." His hips were already moving in excitement. Harley could even feel the heat generating off his body. The energy was electric.

She nodded, "Whatever you say Mister J. You're the boss."

"Y'know, I'm going to explode in that beautiful little mouth of yours." He said and then turned to the nearest guard. "

Wipe down this knife and put it back in the bag. Blind fold the men, but only gag Pam. I want her to watch her beautiful little sister in action. Make sure she has a full view. I want her to see every second."

"You're a fucking sicko, a psycho, a depraved degenerate." Pam began yelling until the guards gagged her with a handkerchief. They followed the rest of his orders without question.

Harley kept her eyes on The Joker but couldn't help herself. "He's a degenerate. You fuck around with every loser cop at Arkham. Mister J is the only real man, you've ever met."

The Joker pet her head, "Don't tell her. Show her. I want her to see how my sexy little kitten pleases her depraved, degenerate God."

Harley licked her bright red lips, pouted and purred. She ran her hands over his backside. He jerked forward as her hands came to the front of his pants.

"Take off your shirt." He demanded.

"Yes, sir." She saluted, took it off and threw it down, playfully. Despite, just killing her father, she felt amazing.

"That's it. Are you gonna take me in your mouth like a good little girl?"

"Yes," she said eagerly licking her lips and running her hand over his cock. "God, you're so hard."

"Show Pam how much you can take - how much you can do. Oh, and how hungry you are? You want to taste me, baby?"

"Yes. Please." She took the zipper of his pants down with her teeth. His cock nearly jumped out with just a slight adjustment from The Joker. "Every time, I see you, oh God." A small tremor rocked her. "You're so beautiful." She licked his shaft and slid her hand around him.

Her yearning lips wrapped around his width and at the same she began working the length with her hands. Mister J rubbed his palm on the top of her head, urging her to take more. She complied.

He grabbed both ponytails and thrust himself into her. He was hard and rough and demanding, but she savored every moment of it.

She took all of him and moved her head quickly back and forth, up and down. She felt herself become wet, but wouldn't dare take her attention off him. She re-positioned herself on the pillow and widened her legs. She began rocking back and forth.

"Naughty, Harley. I like Naughty." Bobbing her head back and forth, she took one hand away to touch her own demanding sex..

"Good girl, right where I showed you baby." She ran her fingers underneath her shorts and inside of her, she pushed hard on her clit. Her moans echoed against his cock. Still, she didn't stop sucking him.

His focus was just on her mouth as he kept going in and out, faster and faster. He felt her tongue roll as she was purring against him and that was enough.

"Yeah, you're such a good little kitten." He held her still and came hard. He saw white drops falling from her mouth to her chest.

He motioned to her and without him saying a word she knew. She licked her fingers and rubbed his seed all over her breasts.

The Joker buckled his pants and let out a few heavy breaths. "See Pam, you could never do anything close to what Harley can." He said, still staring at his blonde-bombshell rocking her pussy. She was sitting with her legs stretched out and riding her hand. She continued with faster strokes until her entire body arched in ecstasy.

"sexy, strong, insatiable." The Joker kept all eyes on Harley. "She's my fucking masterpiece."

She yelled out as her juices spilled on the floor. "M-i-s-t-e-r J"

He waited a few moments, but as her breathing became a bit more normal. The Joker helped Harley stand and motioned to the guard to take off Pam's gag.

"If you were nicer to your sister, I'm sure she would've taught you a few things. You may still have a chance. You just have to understand that Harley and I own you. Maybe, if you're nicer now, she'll let you live. It's her call."

Harley put her shirt back on and listened to Mister J try to repair things with Pam. Harley loved hearing Mister J's eloquent attempt to patch things up, so it made her twice as angry when she heard Pam say. "What the hell is wrong with you? Harley is going to own me? She's a doormat slut who killed our father for a painted up fruitcake."

Harley ran right up to her sister and struck her across the face. "Don't ever disrespect Mister J. He is 1000 times what you and your no-class husband are worth. Do you know how many times your husband tried to kiss me or touch me and I had to tell him to get lost?"

"I didn't know that." The Joker took out his gun and shot him once more. "That's for being ill-behaved."

Harley looked over to the Joker, "Thanks puddin."

"Anything for you, pumpkin."

Harley refocused on Pam. "and then you put down Mister J. For the record, I am not a doormat. I just love listening to what Mister J says because he's always right. He freed me from the madness you call life."

"You're painted up like a clown. All that money invested in becoming a doctor is gone. Dad...." Pam fought back tears, "is gone, and for what? A bad camping trip?"

"Shut up! Shut up. Dad was an abusive asshole who deserved to die."

"He was our father. He put food on our table. He paid for our education. Maybe, he drank too much and raised his hand once or twice, but he wasn't a homicidal maniac!"

"He never abused you, Pam! You sat there and let me take every hit, cut, bruise, slap… he took knives to me and you did nothing! And look at what he did to mom!"

"He did it because you and mom wouldn't listen to him. And what about Tommy? You go from Tommy, a respectable officer who genuinely cared about you to this?" She pointed at the Joker who silently allowed Pam to bury herself. "You slum around with a mass murderer?"

This sent Harley over the edge. She straddled her sister and punched her in the face over and over again. "You'll never change! You'll never get it! You're just like dad! I really wanted you to change! Mr. J is the best thing that ever happened to me and he opened my eyes, but no you still want to stand on your mountain of indignant pride while you and your husband cheat on each other, dad steals from absolutely everyone and we're auctioned off to the highest bidder. You all just lie, cheat and steal and pretend you're the good guys. You're not. Nobody's good, but at least Mr. J admits it. He's honest about it. He doesn't hide who he is. He's magnificent and you can't even see it. He was gonna give you life and you degrade him."

"He's a sociopathic murderer! You are now a murderer! You broke him out of prison and now are giving him dad's millions. He doesn't give a damn about you. He cares about what you can do for him. For God sakes, he had you on the floor giving him fellatio."

"and I enjoyed every second of it. I love him inside of me anytime and anywhere. He's brilliant."

"Can you really look at yourself in the mirror and feel justified?"

"Absolutely. My only regret is that I didn't kill dad sooner."

The Joker watched her fight for a bit enjoying the show and then walked over to Harley. "Come here, kitten. Let's talk."

She got down from her sister and went to him.

"We're not done!" Pam yelled out. "I still have things to say."

"You're done talking to my pumpkin. You're upsetting her." The Joker called back.

He walked a few feet away with Harley. He sighed as if he didn't know what to do. "I say we kill Pam," he said nonchalantly. "She's insulting you. I don't like that."

Harley nodded. "Yeah, and you. How can anyone insult you? Fuck it. We gave her a chance."

"We did. We tried to reason with her, but she refused to respect you or take any responsibility. Blaming you for killing your father….ridiculous."

"Exactly. It was his fault."

"110% kitten. You did everything you could do." He took her in his arms and hugged her while a manipulative smile emerged on his face.

"You always understand me. You're going to go down in the history books as Gotham's Greatest Visionary."

"I hope so. So, we kill Pam?"

She nodded. "Shoot her." She motioned to The Joker's goons. "Shoot her and her stupid husband because I am not going to be explaining myself for the next 50 years and I'm not going to let her put me in jail because she'd snitch on a dime."

When the men didn't act The Joker looked at them. "Do as she says. Do whatever she says. Always." He kept Harley in a tight embrace. "I know this is difficult, but it's almost over. You did an amazing job today. I'm so proud of you."

"I adore you," she looked at him. "I do. I am madly in love with you."

He kissed her hotly and put her hand against his heart. "I heard what Pam was saying out there. I heard what you said too. Don't let her words torment you like your father's did. That's over. You never have to worry about that again. Whenever those voices show up, you just remember this: You are the Queen of Gotham. Anything you say goes. I'll make sure of it."

"Because you're the king,"

"Yeah, the King of Gotham is back and things are going to change around here."

"I can't wait. I just want you to rule the world and come for the ride."

"It's going to be one hell of a ride, baby. Just hold on tight."

They unloaded into Pam and her husband until all you could see was blood, bullets and holes. Then they turned the guns toward Tommy. "What now?"

The Joker looked at Harley. "It's your call. How should little Tommy die? We could give him the easy way out, bullet to the brain – or we could slice and dice him into a trillion unrecognizable pieces."

Tommy was now begging. "No, I didn't do anything. Just let me go and I won't say a word. I swear."

She ignored his pleas and turned to the Joker. "Umm, I kind of wanted to stab him into the trillion pieces, but we just cleaned the knife."

The Joker turned to her and took out the knife he cut Tommy with earlier. "No worries. It's easy to clean a knife. Plus, this one is better. It'll hurt more. See the edges. I'll get you one like this. I'll even engrave it."

"Awww. Mr. J, you make every experience perfect. Thank you," she leaned in and kissed him. "You always think of everything."

Tommy started to panic and tried to free himself. "What? Listen, HARLEY, Harley Quinn, I'm sorry for whatever I did. Please? Why? You don't have to do this."

"You're right, but I want to. The same way you wanted me to marry you knowing I wasn't interested. The same way you stood there while my father beat the shit out of me and threatened my mother. The same way you pounced on me like a teenage virgin knowing I found you detestable. Do you know how many showers I took and how much money I spent throwing out perfectly good clothing because you wouldn't stop touching me or trying to dry-hump me. And you knew, you knew the only reason I went along with it was because I didn't want my mom committed."

The Joker began laughing. "Dry humping you? Gross. Did he ever go further with you?" He had the knife in his hand and tightened the grip.

Harley felt herself grow excited. "He tried, but I said 'no' every time. Told him I had migraines, cramps, anything to get him off of me. He didn't care he just wanted to get off."

"Did he ever get rough with you?"

"No, but he got my father to. He was too much of a pussy to hit me himself so he cried to my father that I wouldn't put out. This is what I got for not fucking the most boring man alive." She raised her head and showed a faded scar where someone sliced ½ way across her neckline.

The Joker just nodded. "Men, I'm giving you a break and a show. Take your seats." He pulled a chair close to him and took Harley by the hand. "For you my dear."

She kissed his cheek and sat.

"So for those of you who weren't paying attention during intermission, we found out some stuff about Officer Redmond. He ran to Harley's father and complained about her. He bribed Harley's father to make her marry him. He tried to buy her which was the wrong thing to do." He turned his focus to Harley. "Baby, who do you belong to?"

"You, Always You." She blew him a kiss.

"That's my girl. Tommy my boy, you shouldn't have tried to take something that wasn't yours. Harley's mine."

"Mr. Joker, I'm sorry, but you didn't even know her then and I didn't know you wanted to be with her."

The Joker cracked up. "Stupid kid," he said motioning to Harley and then turning back to the blindfolded ex. "See, Harley was born to be mine."

Harley closed her eyes and listened to him.

"You think God made her for you? No. She was made in a place much more divine than heaven and by a master much more powerful than God. You didn't have what it takes to excite her or to please her or to get her on her knees begging just to taste you. The very moment you touched her, you were a dead man walking – and now it's time to walk the last mile."

Harley gushed over his words letting out a loving sigh. "Incredible," she simply said.

The Joker began slicing him. He gouged his face, his neck, his chest, his legs, his feet, his arms, his hands. Tommy cried out in pain. The Joker walked over to Harley and handed her the knife. "in and turn, darling. In and turn."

He pulled her close and kissed her hotly. "Do it for me."

She walked over to Tommy who was barely conscious. She jabbed the knife into the first lung and turned. She had to kick Tommy to pull the knife out but did. She then jabbed it into the other one and did the same.

She turned to The Joker "and the show begins."

"The final act," he said with a laugh and sat down bringing Harley to his lap. Tommy died rather quickly and his eyes rolled up into his head.

"After they get the equipment and we get home, you and me are going to have an amazing celebration." The Joker gave her a seductive wink.

"I can't wait. Mister J, I have a favor to ask you."

He turned to her and placed his hands on her shoulder. "Yes pumpkin"

"Can we leave $50,000 here for my mom. I know for a fact, when we find out where Alicia DeAndres lives, my dad gave her at least 2 million cash. She has a ton of gaudy diamonds and a stash of loot she hasn't spent and I'll get you every dime. My mom has had to live week-to-week her whole life, while my dad splurged on his whores."

"We'll definitely find out where Miss DeAndres lives and teach her a lesson. Never let someone betray you and get away with it." He kissed her lips. "and give your mom the fifty. My way of thanking her for helping make my very own sex kitten."

She took the hint and purred for him.

She got up and walked to the kitchen sink. He followed her and looked on as she washed the blood off her body. She shut the water off and turned to him. "When we get home. I want your name on my body. I don't care if you write it with a knife, I just want it there. I want the whole world to see it."

"You want the mark of the beast?" He pulled his shirt to the side and showed her a tattoo of a skeleton wearing a Jester's hat.

"Yes," she moved to it and licked his skin. He held her head still as she danced her tongue on his chest. A near animalistic growl escaped his mouth. He grabbed her roughly and kissed her hard. He was ready to go again and throw her on the table, until Juggles interrupted him.

"They're all dead. Except the mom, of course. She's okay." One of the guys yelled in. "She's in the back room but she's sitting still."

The Joker released Harley and nodded. He motioned for her to go and speak with Mrs. Quinzel. "I'll make it up to you." She whispered in his ear.

"Yes, yes you will." The Joker looked her up and down causing goose flesh to break out on her body.

Harley grabbed 50K and went to her mother.

"Ma, I need you to go to Aunt Christine's and stay with her. I'll check on you when I can, but here's 50 thousand dollars. Don't tell anyone about it. Use this for you. I love you."

Her mother was obviously unstable and nodded. "Okay Harley, it was nice to see you. I love you. Don't stay out too late now."

Harley smiled and then gave her mom a huge hug. "I love you too. Be happy mom. You're free."

Harley walked out of the house, and with all of her strength punched her own arm. 'Don't cry.' she said to herself. 'No weakness.'

The Joker wasn't far behind. "I threw Mommy Quinn another 50K." He whispered in her ear. She turned around and gave him a huge hug.

He moved his finger to her lips as if to keep quiet about it. She just nodded.

"Let's hit the road." The Joker went to help her into a white van, but she stopped. "I said let's go."

"I know and we will - just not in this. I have a present for you." She took out her father's keys from her pocket and opened the garage.

Inside was a hot pink Lamborghini. "He bought it, but never drove it and never registered it. He was too afraid the feds would find out he spent some money he shouldn't have."

"Do you like?"

He walked quickly toward the car with her following behind. The men took the white van and started driving off to the house. Harley quickly put on a red bra and black shorty shorts and threw her bloody clothes in a bag in the back. She jumped in the passenger seat. "So, do you like it or what?"

He ran his hand across the wheel. "This is a nice gift." He tilted his head demanding that she come closer.

"Yes sir" she said and crawled over to him. She placed her hand on his thigh and sat against him. The car went up to 140 and he pushed it to the limit. The faster he drove the hotter she got. She moved her hand from his thigh to her own. He looked down and laughed. "Poor insatiable kitten."

"I can't help it. It's you. Whenever you're close to me, my body demands to be touched."

"Don't help it. I like a good show."

She laid back on the seat and began riding her own hand. The speed of the car, the Joker's presence, the night itself, all made it too much.

The Joker took one hand off the wheel and used his fingers to dance on her skin.

"Mister J,"

"I'm right here,"

"call me your sex toy…"

His eyebrow raised and his voice deepened with a charged passion. "You're my little sex toy, Harley. I wind you up and make you go higher and higher.."

Her entire waist moved up and down as if he were on her. Her breathing grew rapid as she threw her head back in ecstasy. Her hips kept jerking upward.

She stayed there for a moment savoring the sensations.

She sat up and cuddled up to him.

"How did you know?" She whispered.

"Know what?"

"That we would be this way…"

"Because, I saw the devil in your eyes. The same devil that lives in mine."

"So that's it. That why I'm different. I always knew that something in me just wasn't right."

He pulled the car over quick as he nearly missed his driveway. "Nothing is wrong with you. The world is upside down. Life, death, and everything in between is a joke and you get to choose what you live for – what you want." He touched her face lightly.

"I want to live for you"

"I'll make you a deal, you listen to me and I'll make sure everyone listens to you. You'll own the world."

"I want that. I want it all. When we find Alicia, I want to be the one to kill her. The last time I spoke with her and asked her as a 'friend' to stop seeing my father, she was the most condescending…"

"cunt," The Joker smiled.

"Yeah, cunt I've ever spoken with. She criticized my mother. I really want to watch that bitch die. I want to see all of the blood drained from her body. I want the last thing she sees to be me, standing over her with the same knife I killed my father with."

"There you go again," he said turning towards her.

"What?"

"Saying things like that it gets you in trouble." He pushed her down on the seat and laid on top of her.

"I like trouble."

"Let's see how much." He went in the bag and grabbed the hunting knife. He licked the knife drawing blood from his own tongue. He shoved his tongue in her mouth and she kissed him back licking off the blood.

He handed her the knife. Without hesitation, she brought it to her mouth and licked it letting it cut through her skin.

He watched her as he lowered his pants and pulled himself out. He licked the blood from her skin and immediately began grinding himself against her. There was no foreplay. This was about his need and Harley could feel it in his demanding touch.

His hands moved to her shorts and pulled them off her. He widened her thighs and picked her up by her rear. He shoved himself inside of her hard.

"Oh Yeah, treat me like a sex toy, Mister J. You can do anything you want to me."

She knew the words to say to make him insane.

"Stay still, kitten." He used his weight and brute strength to hold her down with one hand and put his other arm on the seat to balance. "Purr for me,"

She purred. He fucked her and at times her body would instinctively try to move against him, but he would tighten his grip. "be still. I just want to fuck you. Be that sex toy. Don't move. Let me just have you."

She forced her body to go against its will and remain near lifeless. "Use me. Play with me. I'm yours to play with."

He fucked her selfishly. It was rough and raw and all sorts of wrong which made him excited all the more. "just my own little sex toy. No one else gets to touch you. You're just mine. SAY IT." He pulled her hair hard so that he was looking in her eyes. His body kept thrusting harder and harder.

"YES! You own me. You can do whatever you want."

He hit her rear hard which startled her. He forced his fingers underneath his cock and inside of her.

She became wet. His narcissistic approach only turned her on more. "Hit me again. Hard."

He raised his hand and slapped her ass again. His grunts of pleasure excited her. She gave herself completely over to him. She let him exploit her body for his own needs. She tightened herself around him to make the experience more over-the-top, but didn't move. His thrusts came faster and harder.

"Come on puddin, anything you want." She said staring him in the eyes.

He looked at her beautiful face and struck it hard. He groaned loudly and came.. He kissed her lips and her tongue instantly wandered into his mouth.

"Good girl," was all he said as he patted her stomach, sat up and put himself back in his pants.

She licked her lips and sat up. She wanted him to know that she enjoyed it. She kissed him hard again. "Thank you, Mister J." She purred.

He ran his hand over her bright white face. "You like being used? You like being treated like a sex toy? You like being slapped?"

"By you? Absolutely."

He nodded and his head fell back against the seat. "You're good at it."

"yeah?"

"Yeah, you understand control – even if you don't know it. You're strong- strong enough to be weak when you need to be. Strong enough to be used."

"Thank you." She said with a sincere smile.

"Let's go inside and watch the news. We have some celebrating to do."

The Joker ordered the men out of the main living room and to the outside porch and front yard to keep a lookout.

Harley brought her bag to the bedroom and took out a red nightie. She took a pair of scissors and ran it up and down to cause frays. She threw it on, tightened her ponytails and refreshed her make-up. She walked out to see the Joker standing by the couch.

"You ok, Mister J."

"the idiots outside left blood on the floor from earlier."

"I'll go get the mop," she said, but he stopped her.

"No. The Queen sits on her throne with the King. We pay people to not fuck up."

She tried not to show herself swoon but her legs buckled in.

"Juggles!" The Joker called out already having the gun in his hand. "Yeah boss…"

"Explain to Harley why there is still blood on the floor."

"Umm, well. I must've missed it. I'm sorry." He took a hanky out of his jacket, knelt down and wiped it up.

The Joker looked at Harley as he cocked the pistol. "Your call."

"It'd just cause more blood. Plus, we have celebrating to do."

The Joker grunted and rolled his head in a circle. "Do you want to say something to Harley?"

"Th..thanks Miss Quinn."

"No worries," she jumped on the couch.

"Go back to your post." Juggles walked out and the Joker strolled over and sat next to Harley. "I like what you did," he said motioning to her negligee.

He turned on the 60-inch TV and put on the news. On the screen, she saw her childhood home.

"Quick coverage…" He said nonchalantly.

"The Quinzel home, once the American Dream has been turned into a nightmare. As reported earlier, It is believed that Dr. Harleen Quinzel was kidnapped by the criminal mastermind known only as The Joker. Either The Joker or members of his gang are believed to have broken into the Quinzel home, robbed them and then murdered Sgt. Benjamin Quinzel, his daughter Pamela Pollock, son-n-law Officer James Pollock and future son-n-law Officer Thomas Redmond. The only known survivor, Mrs. Anne Quinzel has been placed with family at a secure location. She was unable to provide the police with any information on the assailants. If you have any information regarding this heinous crime, please call the Gotham police department at 708-555-6298. Do not try to apprehend The Joker or any member of the gang known as the Circus yourself. He is armed and very dangerous

"Criminal mastermind – I like that…Remind me to send that reporter a gift basket."

"No. She called me Harleen and said I was kidnapped!"

"Okay, we'll kill her then." He said with a smirk. "In her defense, we did kill everyone who could tell them about Harley."

"True, and my mother is okay. The only good thing my father ever taught her was to not talk to reporters or authorities." She sighed. "I just want the world to know I'm with you. I don't want them thinking that …"

"You're helpless or scared?"

"Exactly. I don't want to be depicted as some damsel in distress. I want them to know that I willingly follow you."

"Free will,"

"Free will." She agreed with authority.

"I think I'm going to keep you." He said and rose from his feet. He walked over to her shoulder and gave it a bite. "I'm going to take a shower and then if you're really good, maybe I'll give you a mark or two."

"I could join you in the shower…"

He smiled and placed his hand on her cheek. She moved her head around so that his finger dropped to her lips.

"I want you to wait for me. I want you to crave me." He said in an erotic whisper.

"But I do. I crave you, right now." She knelt before him and licked her lips.

"Don't give in. Don't touch yourself. Don't distract yourself. Just wait. Think about me and wait."

She sat back and let out a near painful sigh. "You punishing me?"

"Oh no, when I punish you. You'll know it. You'll feel it." He took her palm and put small bites on it. "This is just a game."

"Okay Mr. J. I'll wait, but I can only wait so long…"

"poor insatiable kitten." He said mockingly and walked away.

"Don't touch yourself." She said as thoughts of having sex with The Joker wouldn't relent. He took me on the table….in the car…. He used my body….. She could feel herself getting wet and her hand wanted to pet her, but she refused.

"Miss Quinn," Juggles interrupted her thinking. She was actually happy for the distraction as following Mister J's instructions were killing her.

"Yeah,"

"Where's Mr. J?"

"Taking a shower…." She said nonchalantly.

"Well," he sat down aside her. "I just wanted to thank you for helping me earlier."

"No biggie…Everyone makes mistakes."

"It's a big deal to me. You know, Mister J is a very lucky guy to have a gal like you." She suddenly felt too close for comfort and went to get up but Juggles grabbed her hand. "The Joker isn't the only option is what I'm saying."

She snagged her hand back and stood up. "He's the only option for me, and you really shouldn't touch me, at all, ever. Even if you don't mean anything, trust me it can be construed like you do."

Juggles stood up. An entitled look of anger came to his face. "Come on. I know why you helped me earlier. A girl like you, kills her own father, gives the J man a blow job in front of everyone, and then saves me. You want me, just admit it. I know what you're doing with Mister J. I'm just asking for a little taste myself." He pulled her close and received a knee in the groin for his efforts.

"I'm not some bimbo you pass around. I belong to my puddin and no one else!"

"Bitch!" He said and lunged for her. He had her against the wall and was trying to kiss her as she fought back.

"Mr. J is so going to kill you and I can't wait to see it!" She said and spit in his face.

"You think so. I say he needs me more than he needs you. I've been by his side for a decade. You think you're better than me because you're a doctor. You think the Joker is better than me. He's using you and will throw you away like the trash you are." He began to unbutton his suit jacket. "I'll show you what a real man is."

"STOP!" She punched him hard and didn't stop. She kicked him and using a few things she learned in self-defense she was able to keep him at bay. By this time, he was calling her every name in the book.

A gunshot was fired and Harley noticed Juggles was bleeding from the leg.

She looked behind her and saw him standing there. "Puddin," she ran to his arms out of breath. He was already in a sharp silk purple shirt and black pants.

"Did Juggles interrupt our little game?" He asked Harley tapping her back lightly. His eyes were fiery and his tone was dark.

"Yes he did." Harley said still trying to catch her breath.

"That wasn't nice. Juggles what do you have to say for yourself."

"Mister J, this isn't…listen, we go back. We go back far and this …this… Harley..she got in your head and then she got in my head. You know, she was sitting on the couch practically naked begging for it being all flirtatious"

The Joker shot him in his other leg and took a deep breath. "Begging for it? Begging for you?" He asked.

"Stop, please. I'm telling you I don't think she cared who it was. I mean look at the way she was in front of her sister and her family. She'll do anyone anywhere."

"That's not true, pudd-" The Joker raised his hand to silence her.

"Everything she's done has been with me. Now, when I came out, she looked very uninterested. You were bleeding and she was fighting back pretty hard."

"Mister J, you know how girls are. Some play hard to get and that's all it was. I mean, I'm sorry. Okay, I'm sorry that she got under my skin like that but look at her. You have great taste in women so you can't fault a guy for wanting to get in on that."

The Joker shot him in his arm. "Sorry? You're sorry." He lifted his head keeping Juggles in his peripheral vision. "Kitten, were you playing hard to get with Juggles?"

"NO. Never. He tried to touch me on the couch and I told him I was yours. I told him not to touch me. He said that he was better than you. He was trying to rape me." She punched her arm with all her strength not to cry.

"Juggles, Juggles, Juggles" The Joker sighed and shot him in his other arm. "Maybe, I should go to the surveillance videos? What would I see? Would I see my devoted little sex kitten that broke me out of Arkham, jumped into a vat of acid and told me where all the money her family had was, come on to you – or would I see you touching her. The problem with a bum like you is that you don't understand the difference between foreplay and rape. You don't understand that the whole purpose of control is consent. I own Harley because Harley wants to be owned. But more than all of that I HATE RAPISTS!"

Juggles was near tears. "No. Okay. Please, I'm sorry. I'm sorry Harley. Okay. I just got out of control."

"it's your call." The Joker wanted to kill him. He wanted to watch his blood spill, but this one had to be Harley's. he knew what she was going to do. He wanted her to do it. It was a gift from him to her. He was giving her the power to make Juggles pay for his sins.

She walked over to the Joker and took the gun from his hand. She shot Juggles until there were no more bullets. She raised her head up and took a deep breath. "I'll get the mop."

"No. The Queen sits on the throne with the King." He kissed her forehead. "Go in the bedroom and wait for me. I'm going to have North come in here and get rid of this bum."

She turned around and began walking to the room.

"You ok?" He asked with his head down.

"I am." She said with all the confidence she could muster.

"I should have made him suffer more. Lost at my own game."

"What?" she asked confused.

"I couldn't wait. The thought of him touching you, anyone touching you...."

Harley turned and ran to him. "I didn't want that, ever. He disgusts me."

"I know." The Joker said softly. "I won't leave you alone with anyone again."

She leaned up and kissed him. She licked his lips and urged them open with her tongue. He fell into it and kissed her back. He was soon in control and pulled her close. He moved his mouth to her neck and began biting and leaving marks on her body.

"Puddin,"

"Yeah,"

"Fuck me right here. Right now." She lowered herself to the floor and sat down.

He took off his purple shirt and hung it over the couch. She loved the tattoos that covered his body. They were gorgeous. Everything about him was amazing.

He got on the floor with her and pushed her down.

She purred into his ear. "You make everything disappear. You make everything perfect."

"It's your turn," he said as he stripped her naked. "No need to wait this time." His hand went directly in-between her legs. She opened her thighs, leaned her head back and exposed herself fully to him. He raked his forefinger over her. She was already wet. He spread her legs further apart and put his mouth on her. He flicked his tongue against her sex.

She pushed herself instinctively up and moaned uncontrollably. "Keep purring" he said softly.

She brought her head back and did so. His tongue entered her and touched her spot immediately. She rocked back and forth. She placed her legs on his back. "Yes, Yes, Yes, Yes, YES…. " her body slowly relaxed as small pulsations rocked her. She put her hand through his hair and purred once more.

The Joker sat up and looked at Juggles. He started laughing.

She laughed a bit without even knowing why. His joy brought her joy.

He reached for his gun and took a bullet out of his shirt and placed it in the chamber. He shot Juggles dead body. "I don't like people watching."

Harley started laughing hysterically. He took her hand and licked it. "My amorous little sex toy can fight."

"Yes, she can." Harley said with pride.

"You didn't learn that in gymnastics." He said dancing his fingers in hers.

"I took a self-defense course when I started working at Arkham."

The Joker rose and provided his hand. "Stand up. Let's go put my mark all over that sexy little body of yours."

She purred in excitement. "I want you everywhere." She ran her hand from the top of her neck to her waist and center.

"Go get on the bed. I'm gonna get North and have him take care of this clown." He pointed to Juggles and they both cracked up.

She picked up her nightie and walked into the bedroom.

"Don't put anything on."

She dropped the nightie down in obedience and went onto his bed. She laid on her stomach naked. He could see her shadow from where he stood. He took the view in for a second and then went to retrieve North.

He walked in the room only moments later. He had his purple shirt back on but unbuttoned. He closed the door behind him and strolled over to a record player. He took out an album and put it on. The tune had a malevolent, shadowy sound with no lyrics. It was perversely erotic.

He went to his closet and swung the door open. Harley looked over and saw all sorts of weapons and metallic tools that she didn't recognize. He took out a tattoo gun.

"No peeking," he said and closed the door.

He sat beside her on his bed.

"I gotta question, Mister J?"

"ask it and I might answer it."

"Why do you ask me to purr…" Just to show she wasn't making a power-play, she purred after she spoke.

"because, I like when you do things I say."

She laughed and purred again. "I was just wondering because in Arkham I heard there was this gal they were trying to catch named.."

"Catwoman," he said as he turned on the tattoo gun.

"Yeah, she thinks she's a cat or something."

"Pumpkin, are you asking if I ask you to purr because I have a thing for another?"

"Um, well yeah. I guess so."

"Would it bother you? He pressed the tattoo gun against her back and she didn't flinch as he began his work.

"I guess it would Mister J. I mean, I like it 'just us' you know."

"You're in luck then. I don't much have a thing for cats or gals that find bats attractive. I like little sex kittens. I like my little sex kitten. Purr for me"

She let out a naughty sigh and then looked at him. She kept her mouth slightly open so he could see her tongue rolling as she purred.

He knelt behind her, his hardening crotch against her rear as he tattooed her back against the bone. She kept her back as still as she could but pushed her bottom so she could feel him even more. "be still kitten. We'll play soon enough."

The Joker was astonished by her threshold for pain. He knew how it felt. He knew it hurt, but his brave sexy Harley looked as if she was getting a massage.

After he was done, a large skeleton with a Jester's hat took up the middle of her back and her upper shoulder said "property of Joker" as promised. The ink and the blood were mixing. He rubbed his hands over it and then licked it off. He taped up her back.

"Done already?" She asked.

"Not even close pumpkin. Flip over."

She giggled and did so. He rubbed her legs and then picked up his tattoo gun once more. He didn't turn it on but just ran it against her center. She opened her legs.

He pushed the side of it against her sex and she began riding it. She would get closer to the needle with each circular motion.

"You're going to cut yourself," he said with a smile.

"I'm your bad little sex toy. Punish me." She began to move even quicker, "Put in me, please." She was out of breath.

He did so and let it pierce the inside of her. She rode it like it was a jackhammer rubbing her hand all around it. Her climax rocked her hard. "That's it. Oh Mister J."

He let out a guttural groan and withdrew the gun. He licked her wetness off of it. "I like wild and I love crazy. You are something else entirely."

He placed his gun below her stomach and on the top of her shaved skin wrote out Mister J

"Mister J" she said with a smile. "That's perfect. You're amazing at everything."

"Everything that matters." He ran his tongue over each letter. A small erotic sound escaped her lips.

He moved down to her legs and covered them with his markings and phrases.

Then on her forearm arm over the scar her father had left, he created diamond shapes connected in red and black. He then touched her face. Underneath her eye, he put a small heart. It was in the same place where on his face he had a tear drop J. He bent down and kissed her face and then the last tat simply said "rotten" on the side of her cheek

He put the gun down and took a deep breath. "do you even feel pain," he said softly.

"Yes. But I like your kind of pain" she said and placed her leg on each side of him. He kissed her leg and then bit it hard. She just giggled in excitement.

He threw off his shirt, and unbuttoned his pants. He pushed them off and positioned himself right on top of her. He rubbed the blood and ink from her skin all over her breasts. His mouth traveled up to her neck. He took a fierce grip on her thigh and pulled it over him.

"So, you like pain."

She nodded.

Instinct took over and he let the animal inside of him out. He entered her fully and a moan escaped her lips.

"Does that hurt?" He asked between breaths.

"Yeah," she managed to get out.

"You want more?"

"Yes," she smiled and pushed her waist up against him.

Sounds of intense rapture escaped him. He held her leg up to get even deeper. He took his other hand and shoved his fingers inside as he thrust. He could feel her tear, but still she pushed against him.

"my very own masochist. I always wanted one." he said forcing his hand all the way into her.

She just extended her leg further. "Don't stop." She said as she grabbed a hold of the headboard and tightened herself against him. "Fuck me…."

He reached to the table and grabbed one of his hand guns. He ran it against his lips and then hers. She took it in her mouth as if it were his cock as she continued to fuck him.

"Fearless, You're so fearless Harley," He pushed her to the edge as he began to reach his own depraved bliss.

She screamed out as her whole body began to shake in a near seizure. She felt him come in her as he let out a long primal groan. He threw the gun across the room and sat up. He put his hand through his slick hair.

He touched her face.

"You gonna keep me, puddin?" She asked with a smile.

"you're not going anywhere."

She smiled. "You know Mister J. I dreamed about this when I was a little girl."

"You dreamed that you'd be with me?"

"No, I dreamed that I'd be with someone who would let the whole world burn to save me, a man who would put himself above anyone else and let me come for the ride – not just as his girlfriend, but as a participant. This, here with you, is what I've always wanted."

He laughed. "You were born to be Harley Quinn."

She sat up and kissed him. "I was born to be yours."

"Well then, now you have the marks to prove it." He ran his fingers over her body. "You go shower off and come to bed. We have a big day tomorrow."

"What's tomorrow?" She said eagerly.

He pointed to the bathroom. "Patience, doll-face."

She pouted but got up and headed toward the bathroom.

"Don't worry pumpkin. You'll enjoy it."

She turned back, "I always do."

Once she was in the shower he leaned back on the bed. He started laughing. "Tomorrow the world is going to meet Harley Quinn – and I can't wait to introduce her to Batsy."

The Joker was definitely accustomed to sleeping alone, but he didn't push Harley away when she curled up against him.

The next morning, he was already awake when she woke up. "Puddin," she wiped her eyes.

"Get up and get dressed. We got work to do. I need you to make a phone call."

"What? Why?" She yawned and stretched. He didn't say anything, but she saw him tilt his head to the side and was reminded that he didn't like being questioned.

"Sorry, Mister J. Don't know where that came from." She jumped up without saying another word and grabbed a revealing red tank top and a short black skirt that showed more than they covered. She put her bright red lipstick on and nodded as if to say that she was ready.

He took out a cell phone and handed it to her. "I have Alicia's number." He handed her the piece of paper. "You call and say you escaped from me and that you can't go to the police because some are crooked and work for me. You tell her that you have a lot of money from your father and that I'm looking for you and the money. Say that you don't forgive her but right now you need a safe place where I won't think to look. Tell her you'll split the money with her if she lets you come by. Get the address from her." She went to dial but he stopped. "Make it sound real. Can you do that, baby?" He ran his finger against her bottom lip.

She smiled and licked it. "Yes," she said confidently.

"What a good little kitten. Purr for daddy." He rubbed her chin.

She purred.

"Make your call."

"I need you to hit me, first."

His eyes grew wide and he began to flex out his fingers as if struggling to not hit her. "Oh sweet Harley, as enticingly erotic as that sounds…."

"I didn't mean it as foreplay although it does sound like fun." She said with an inviting smirk. "It'll just help me to sound upset so Alicia believes me. Please Mister J. I can take it. Just hit me hard across the face."

There may have been an alternative, but he wasn't looking for one. With an open palm, he struck her hard across her face as a lustful groan escaped his lips. She felt blood trickle out of her mouth. She wiped it away nonchalantly.

He motioned for her to stand, licked the blood off her hand and then licked her lips. "Make the call." He walked behind her, sat on the bed, undid his pants, exposed himself fully and roughly pulled her to his lap where he was fully aroused.

"Should I wait on the call?" She asked moving herself against him.

"Don't worry pumpkin, I'll get rough if I need you need to sound in pain."

"Yes sir," she began dialing as he began gnawing on her neck.

"What if I just want you to get rough?" She moved her body on his.

"Make the call." He already had himself against her grinding.

It was only a few moments before she picked up.

"Hello," There was Alicia's voice.

'I hate this, bitch.' – Harley thought to herself,until she felt Mister J slide lift her skirt and tear her panties aside. Then she didn't care about anything else. She couldn't help but let out a groan, when he entered her hard and raw.

"Umm, um, don't hang up. This is Harleen. I was hurt pretty bad by The Joker…" she began

"not yet, but soon," The Joker whispered against her skin.

"Well, I escaped and I need a place to hide. I can't go to the cops because it was one of them that helped The Joker escape and helped kill my father and Tommy."

Mister J held her waist still as he kept thrusting into while she spoke. She worried Alicia could hear her uncontrolled moans.

"Oh, there's no escape." He said as she bounced despite how forceful his grip was. "Keep going. Keep talking." he said to her.

"I know we don't see eye-to-eye but after what happened to my dad. It's nuts. I know The Joker's gang won't think about you or your house. I, um…" she let out a small sound as he didn't stop. He was unrelenting.

"I have money. Tons. I haven't even counted it yet, but it's millions. I'll split it with you if you let me hide out."

She knew Alicia was thinking about it and Harley gladly gave her the time, using the few free moments to fuck Mister J back.

He laid back with his hand on her spine now grasping to the shirt she was wearing. He moved his hips and her sex began twitching against him.

"Well, okay. If you split the money with me 60/40, you can stay here until they catch The Joker. I'm sure Bat-Man will get that freak anyways."

"Okay," Harley said softly. "Deal. What's the address?"

"612 London Bridge Lane,"

Usually, she'd be pissed at Alicia for demanding a higher split, living in a good neighborhood and just existing, but right now, she just wanted to be off the phone with her full attention on him.

"I'll be here at noon. Meet me then. Go through the garage on the right. There's no cars in that one." Alicia continued.

"I'll be there," Harley hung up the phone and tossed the cell across the room.

The Joker took this opportunity to change positions. He put her on her stomach so that her chin was against a pillow. With her backside facing him and her waist in his hand, he stood behind her and entered her again. He pushed harder and harder. He was grunting in ways she had never heard before. It was possessive, obsessive and near demonic. She reveled in it.

He kept pounding her over and over and she pushed back just as hard. He slapped her on the rear reddening the skin.

"I want control," He said and then pulled her up by the hair. She was now in front of him, staring at herself in the mirror across the room. He went under her shirt and raked his hands over her breasts. He squeezed her nipple in-between two fingers which brought her to the breaking point. "Look at yourself. Watch yourself cum. You're mine Harley. Whatever I want to do to you, I can."

Her body tensed up and small moans escaped her. She watched in the mirror as his cock kept entering her. She widened her legs and lifted so she had a better view. The rush was never-ending. It was like she couldn't catch her breath but didn't care. She'd rather die than have the moment end.

Rather than allow his release, The Joker turned her around so she was staring right in his eyes. She wrapped her legs around his back and he pushed himself inside of her once more.

"Tell me to hit you again."

She spoke to him in a dark twisted tone. "Hit me, Mr. J. Please. I've been so bad." She said moving her hips back and forth. He pulled back his arm this time and hit her hard. She would have fallen off his lap had his other arm not been holding her tightly.

'YESSSSSSS....' she cried out as she felt another orgasm hit her at the same time that the sting of his slap did.

He slapped her on the other side of her face just as hard and then pushed her down to the bed. He was on top of her and bucking his hips with such intensity.

He pinned both her arms down with his other hand. "Now, fuck me back. Be a good girl."

She pushed herself against him over and over. She felt his body gyrating and pulsating against her. "that's it," he breathed into her ear and then bit her neck.

He let out a deep groan of pleasure as he came in her hard. When he withdrew himself, he took her by the wrist and ran her own fingers against her. She flinched from the touch. He then brought her hand to her mouth.

"There you go kitten, drink your milk."

She licked and sucked her own fingers tasting both of their juices together.

"That's it. Now show me your appreciation. Purr for me,"

She purred for him as a few bruises began to make their way on her face. He kissed them softly. He rose from the bed and fixed his pants and straightened his shirt.

"I'll bring the car around. Just fix yourself up a bit and be out in 5,"

"Yes sir."

"Two of my favorite words," He gave her a smile and walked out the door.

She readied herself quickly and then jumped into the passenger side of the pink Lamborghini. With two minutes to go," he said and took one last drag of a cigarette before throwing it.

"You're going to drive your car." He handed her the keys. "Go inside with this bag," He handed her a bag with about 25k in it. "so if she asks for any money up front, you can show her this. You have her lead you into the house. I'll be right behind. It may take me a few if there's an alarm I need to disable."

"You won't have to disable it. If she does have an alarm or a safe the code will be 091392. It's her birthday – she's a narcissist."

"So am I"

"Yeah, but you can make a woman come just by looking at them. You deserve every bit of ego you own."

"Can't argue with that," he giggled and she laughed too.

"Let's go have some fun."

She gave him a quick kiss goodbye.

CHAPTER 02

She drove to Alicia's house and parked in the garage she was told to. When she walked out, she spotted The Joker's cool pink Lamborghini turning the corner. She rang the doorbell and waited for Alicia.

It only took a few moments for Alicia to open the door. She had changed dramatically since high-school. Alicia now wore designer clothing and expensive excessive jewelry. She looked like a cross between Paris Hilton and Mr. T.

Harley fought the instinct to kill her right there, take every piece of jewelry and force it down her throat.

Alicia motioned for Harley to come in and then stared her up and down.

"Damn, you weren't kidding. What'd that Rocky Horror reject do to you? You're all white and those tattoos are disturbing."

"He branded me." Harley answered while thinking 'Fuck you. These tats are awesome.'

"That's one screwed up clown!" Alicia pushed her puffy blonde hair behind her ears. "You got the cash?"

"Yeah, in this bag. I'll give it to you don't worry."

"Okay, then come on."

When she turned around, Harley reached for her cell phone and texted The Joker.

No alarm. Door unlocked.

Alicia looked back and caught glimpse of her using the phone.

"Just letting my mom know I'm okay. She's staying with my aunt." she said as she walked into the three-story, newly built house that no doubt Sgt. Quinzel had purchased.

She put the cash on the long white chaise and then sat aside it.

"Honey, that's décor, obviously. Sit on the couch like a normal person."

Alicia gave a fake smile and sat down. "No offense, but I have got to say, it figures that The Joker would leave your mother alive. She's probably crazier than he is. It's so insane. I can't believe your father is dead. I was sort of hoping your mother would croak first because then I'd get more in the will, but things have a way of working out." She smiled and reached for the bag.

"That they do," His crackling voice was unmistakable. There, he was. He stood tall in her living room. He had a long purple snakeskin jacket, a silver shirt and black pants. His eyes revealed that the smile on his lips meant nothing. He was holding a Glock 41 and pointing it right at her.

"He must've tracked you, you stupid bitch!" Alicia looked at Harley.

Harley stood up proudly, took her bag and walked up to The Joker. He pulled her close with his free arm and kissed her hotly.

"Good job, pumpkin."

"What the hell is going on?" Alicia stood up and backed up nearly falling into her fireplace.

"I'd stay still if I were you." The Joker's tone was ice cold.

"Harleen, you told me that you were on the run from him."

"She lied to you. I gave her your number, I told her to call and I was fucking her while she was talking to you." He turned to Harley. "Remember that?"

"The memory is burned into my mind." She cuddled close to him and licked his ear. "Everything you do is burned in my mind."

"Harleen, I don't get it! Tell me what the hell is going on!" Alicia was stammering.

Harley let out a sigh and turned to her. "First, the name isn't Harleen. it's Harley now – Harley Quinn. Second, you need to keep up. I lied to you. Mister J and I came here to get what was ours. I want the money my father gave you."

"That's what this is about. You're still upset about me and your dad? He pursued me. Okay. If anything, be pissed at him. You paired up with the guy who killed your father to get revenge on me?" That's insane!"

"I killed my father." She said sternly.

The Joker leaned against her. "And you did a really good job."

"Oh my god! Okay, I'll give you the money but just leave okay. I won't tell the cops I saw you."

The Joker laughed. "I don't think you understand how this works. We can either torture you to death or we can make it quick and easy. He took out a knife from his pocket with the other hand and handed Harley the gun.

"Um, you don't have to do that. I'm sorry. I was just surprised and taken aback and a little scared and I didn't know what was going on." Alicia suddenly stopped for a moment, took a deep breath as if she was about to walk on stage and then pouted her lips and batted her eyes. "Please, I'll give you the money. Just don't hurt me. I'll do anything you want."

"Fucking whore…" Harley said under her breath.

"Now, now pumpkin, let's hear her out." The Joker walked over with the knife. He sat beside her and placed the weapon against her cheek. "You want to prove your loyalty, start with this. Where's the money?"

She went to speak but he placed the knife on her lips. "Now remember, you can't spend it if you're dead. And you should know that I'm aware of how much you have so if there's more than one place, it's wise to tell me."

Alicia nodded. "Of course Mr. Joker, most of it is under my mattress in my bedroom, I have more in a box in the closet in the bedroom. It's on the top shelf. I have another $250,000 in the cabinet to the right of the sink in the kitchen. Then I have a couple thousand in my purse."

Harley started laughing. "Wow Alicia, great hiding places. No one would ever think to look under your mattress."

The Joker chuckled. "Pumpkin, I want you to go get our money and I'll stay here and talk to Alicia and find out what she's willing to do for us."

As much as Harley wanted to rip Alicia's head off, she complied. "You're the boss, Mister J." She walked over and handed him the gun.

"That I am." He watched Harley as she walked away. She collected the money silently reassuring herself that The Joker was merely playing with Alicia and she'd be dead soon.

"Okay, I'm listening. What do you think you could possibly bring to me or to The Circus? What do you have to offer?"

"What are you looking for?" She asked seductively. "I can pretty much do whatever you need me to do. I'll tell you that Harleen- I'm sorry, Harley's dad never complained once."

"That's cute. You think you're good enough for me or do you think I'll just fuck any pussy put in front of me?"

"No, of course not. I'm sure we could figure out something though. We could even bring Harley into it. I mean, I can get pretty crazy."

He raised his head and laughed and Alicia let out a victorious giggle as well. He moved a little closer and then said softly. "So you can offer the average man's dream – watching two women go at it. Now, tell me, do I look like the average man?"

"No, not at all. I'm sorry. I just don't know what you're looking for. If you tell me, I can be it."

Harley was now out with all the money in a bag. She put it down and looked at the Joker. "another 3.5 here. Looks like my dad was very generous."

"He must've turned his head to a lot of really bad stuff." The Joker glanced at the cash, "and I'm glad he did. Come here pumpkin, come sit down." He tapped the chaise.

She listened to him and sat. "Alicia had declared that this was décor and that I couldn't sit on it."

"Oh, well we're slowly but surely teaching Alicia who is in charge. Alicia you should apologize to Harley." He ran the knife over her neck.

"I'm sorry about everything."

Harley didn't even acknowledge it. "So, what'd I miss?"

"Well, we have another contestant wanting to play my favorite game: Let's Make a Deal. She offered to do anything I asked her to do, including fucking you in front of me."

"Oh how risqué," Harley and The Joker laughed aloud. "I was just telling her that I wasn't an average man, and I certainly don't have average needs."

"Yeah, but your needs are my needs." Harley smiled and licked her lips.

The Joker walked to the chaise, tossed his jacket on a nearby chair and sat behind Harley. He handed her the gun. "Keep that on our hostage," he whispered. "Now Alicia, a lot of bizarre and twisted things arouse me. See these marks," He turned Harley's face from left to right showing the bruises. "Tell our friend how you got those,"

The Joker moved one hand under her shirt as he squeezed her breast. The other dove directly between her legs. She opened them on instinct and started moving against his hand. "Mister J likes it rough," she said now riding his four fingers. He pushed her panties aside and fondled her in front of Alicia's whose face was now reddening.

"Do you like it when daddy gets rough?" He pulled Harley on top of him. He was hard and demanding in his touch.

"You know I do, daddy," she said grinding her body in his lap.

Alicia turned her head away and closed her eyes. The Joker unzipped his pants and lowered them until he was fully exposed. He ran his hand up her chest and onto her neck, lightly choking her. "Alicia wants to know what turns me on so we're going to show her."

"Sounds like fun,"

He pulled Harley onto him quick and hard. "I'm going to make you come for me, so you may want to make sure, she can't run away."

Without missing a beat and before Alicia could digest the words, Harley put a bullet in each leg. Alicia rolled to her side and screamed out in pain.

The Joker bit Harley's neck hard in approval. "See Alicia, Harley has great timing, she's a great shot and she'd really do anything for me. Come on Alicia, open your eyes. If you don't listen to me, Harley's just gonna kill you now. Open your eyes and see what you're up against."

Alicia swallowed hard as tears streamed down her face. She struggled to sit up and then opened her eyes.

Harley picked herself up to give Alicia the full show. Shen then mounted herself right onto his engorged cock. She began riding him as he moved his hands all over her body, driving her crazy.

"Let's play a game. Would you ever tell me no, Harley?"

"Never" his fingers pushed her center while she controlled every thrust with her body contracting on him.

"Yeah, what if I wanted to fuck you during a church service."

"Oh God, I'd want to be in the front row."

"What if I wanted to hit you, huh? What if I just wanted to hit you so hard that it took your breath away." He turned her head gently to him, kissed her softy and then slapped her face forward.

"Harder," she said as she quickened her pace.

He pushed her down on the chaise and got on top of her. He held her by the shoulders and took control. "What if I told you I was going to kill you?" She knew what answer he wanted.

"I'd beg you to fuck me first."

"What would you say?"

"Please daddy, if you're going to kill me let me just feel you. Let me just taste you." She reached the peak and moaned out.

He withdrew himself and got onto his knees, pulling Harley up by her ponytails. "Taste me." He demanded.

She licked her lips and then put him in her mouth. She began sucking him. He put his hand behind her head and fucked her as if he was still inside her sex. His grunts were violent and demanding. He reached his apex quickly and held Harley still as he flooded her with his seed. She eagerly swallowed every drop.

He took her hand in his and licked it. "You want to kill the Sgt's whore?" He asked as her body began to twitch at the thought.

"YES, Please, Let me do it."

"What are you going to do?"

By this time Alicia was protesting but they didn't hear her. The Joker kept her in his peripheral vision to make sure she wasn't trying to crawl away, but otherwise, Harley and Mister J were locked in ecstasy.

"In and turn, just like daddy taught me."

"That's my girl. Go get her." He buttoned his pants and sat up turning to Alicia. "I'm sorry but after much consideration, we've decided to go a different direction. You're just not a right fit for The Circus." The Joker and Harley began laughing aloud.

"Come on, Harley. We went to school together. We grew up together. Don't do this!"

"God I hate when people beg for their lives. It's so boring. Harley show the world what this woman really is. Make her look on the outside the way she is on the inside," he extended his hand as if giving Alicia to her. "Have fun, pumpkin."

Harley got up and walked over to Alicia who was hovering against the couch. "Stop it. Please. I gave you the money."

"This was never about money. The money was a bonus, but I came here for one reason and that's to kill you." She began just slashing Alicia, cutting through her skin. Alicia attempted to struggle so The Joker rose. He threw his shirt on a chair, walked behind Alicia and held her hands above her head.

"Come now, you said you'd do anything I wanted. I want to watch you die." He said laughing. "Go ahead Harley. Do whatever you want."

The mixture of the Joker's heat and her desire to watch Alicia die overtook her. She quivered again on the inside and let out a small moan. She then held the knife and stabbed Alicia the way The Joker showed her. She stabbed her over and over and over again, jabbing it in, twisting it and pulling it out, jabbing it in, twisting it and pulling it out.

She didn't stop until Alicia was motionless and not breathing. The Joker had dropped her hands and walked over to Harley. "I don't think anything gets me hotter than seeing you in the blood of your enemies."

She wrapped her arms around him and kissed him. Her tongue wandered in his mouth as he lowered her to the floor.

He removed her shirt and took a nipple in his mouth while her hands unbuckled his pants. "How'd that feel? Huh, taking her life."

"Amazing," she said using her legs to lower his pants and running her fingers through his hair.

He ripped her panties off and tossed them aside. She pushed her body up against his hard member.

"Insatiable" He mumbled against her. Her body kept urging him in. He teased her. He placed the tip against her wet sex and slid it up and down.

Her neck dropped back against the floor. "I want you baby. I need to be yours." The Joker licked and sucked on her neck. He put small bites and ownership marks on her. "Please – please Mr. J."

He reached on the chaise and grabbed his Glock. He lowered it to her pussy and ran it on her wetness. She pushed herself down rocking herself against the barrel of the gun.

"I have my hand on the trigger. It could go off at any time." The Joker said darkly.

"I don't care,"

The Joker laughed, he withdrew the pistol, threw it aside and entered her hard.

"That's it. There it is. You belong in me." Her nails dug into his back as he pounded her against the marble floor.

The Joker's eyes were intense watching every twitch, every move, every moment of euphoria and rapture hit Harley. He reveled in it. "Purr for me," he demanded.

She rolled her tongue, but her purrs were interrupted by pleasure filled moans of gratification.

He hungrily kissed her, letting his tongue wander inside her mouth.

His movements quickened and became more forceful. Craving sounds of possessiveness and indulgence escaped his lips.

She licked his mouth, "That's it, puddin. I want you. I want to feel you. I belong to you. My body is yours." He felt her tense against him and she bit onto his back as his rhythm brought her to new heights and a moment of heaven washed over her.

He thrust a few more times and then climaxed hard.

He laid on top of her for a bit. "I can hear your heartbeat against me," she whispered.

"I don't have a heart." He laughed and she joined in.

"Well whatever is beating against me, I like it."

"You like everything about me," he stood up and pulled her up. He massaged her neck.

"I love everything about you." She said giving him a quick kiss. "Thank you so much for letting me kill this bitch. It was very therapeutic for me."

The Joker laughed. "You know, I'd do anything for you, kitten."

She purred for him. "Where next, puddin?"

"We have a date at The Gotham Fundraising event of the season. Tonight the most successful people in Gotham will all be at the Waldorf eating expensive cuisine and donating like crazy to get Mayor Marion Grange reelected."

"That sounds like a party, I'd like to crash."

"Well you're in luck doll-face, because tonight is Harley Quinn's coming out party.

CHAPTER 03

It was 5 o'clock. All the customers had left. Christine Lemon, the owner of Lacey's Club Cross was happy to see the day end. She had to go and get ready for the Waldorf.

She walked over to the door with the keys in her hand and saw The Joker, 4 henchmen and a woman she didn't recognize walking to the door. Christine rushed with the keys, but it was no use.

The Joker shot the lock off and began laughing. He stood in front of her wearing a black tuxedo with a white bowtie.

Christine backed off with her hands up. As the woman got closer, Christine saw that it was the missing girl mentioned on the news. It was Dr. Harleen Quinzel.

"Oh, I think you have a couple more minutes. It's my lady's big night." The Joker held the door for Harley who kissed him on the cheek and walked in.

"It's my coming out party," she said. "The name is Harley Quinn. Nice to meet ya."

Christine just nodded. North walked over to her, patted her down, took her cell phone and advised her to sit in a chair. She did.

Harley meanwhile walked through the store looking at all the designer clothing. The Joker wasn't far behind. "Spare no expense. We have a gift card," he pointed at the henchmen holding guns. "Just get something hot and call me when you're ready to show it off."

"Of course," she smiled and browsed through the clothing. She came across a short red dress with a V neck that fell passed the breasts and down to the stomach. The shoulder straps crisscrossed in the back. There was a slit up the side. She grabbed a pair of black fishnet stockings, a bright red bra with matching thong panties, and a pair of red pumps.

She went to the dressing room and put everything on. She touched up her lipstick, tightened her ponytails and then called out. "Mister J, you want to check out what I picked?"

He walked over to the fitting area. She slowly opened the door and then stood against the wall. "What do you think, Puddin?"

He tilted his head and looked her up and down. She recognized the dark look of lust in his eyes. She slid her hand from her neck, downward.

"Too bad we only have a few minutes," she said and licked her lips.

"Don't move" he ordered. He walked back over to Christine and shot her dead. "Wait in the van," he told the men. He took the keys and locked the door behind them. He took off his jacket, loosened the bow-tie, and unbuttoned his shirt. He then returned to Harley, only stopping to grab two belts. One was pure leather and the other was made of rope.

"Welcome back,"

"I got us some more time. It seems that the owner doesn't care how late we stay."

Harley laughed aloud. She saw the belts he had in his hand. "Should I be worried?"

"Yes," he said with only a hint of smirk, deep down in the corner of his eye. "Give me your hands."

She put them in front of him, one on top of the other crisscross at the wrist.

"Good girl," he spoke softly as he wrapped the rope around her hands tightly. He then raised her arms and hung them on the clothing hook behind her.

He ran his fingers down the front of her body. He put his knee in between her thighs and pushed the bottom of her dress up. He tore her stockings apart and ripped the new panties off. He rubbed his hand against her rear and then gave it a hard slap.

She trembled.

He unbuckled his pants and leaned against her. He was already rock hard and ready to play.

"You like being tied up?" He asked taking her legs and draping one on each side of his waist. His engorged cock rested against her wet twitching sex.

"Yes," her voice cracked. Anticipation and desire controlled her every cell. "I want you."

"My poor insatiable sex kitten. Purr for me."

She rolled her tongue and made the sound he craved to hear. He kissed her deeply owning her mouth, gnawing on her lips, drawing blood with his teeth.

He broke the kiss to look her straight in the eyes. "How depraved are you, my sweet?" His tone was sinister and wicked. The Cheshire grin he wore was that of a possessed fiend.

She could only imagine what type of debauchery he had up his sleeve. Whatever it was, she was in. "As depraved as you can imagine," she answered.

"Let's hope so," he raised the other belt for her to see. He wrapped it around her neck and waited. He waited to see if she'd stop him. She didn't. "such a good girl," he said and clasped it. She could barely breathe and all she could smell was leather.

'Every time I think I've seen it all, he revs it up harder, hotter' she thought to herself.

He had one hand on her rear and the other was holding the end of the belt in a fist against her waist.

"You like this?" He asked giving the belt a slight tug.

"Yes," she moved her body against him. Her sex was nearly dripping she was so wet. His cock felt like a sword stabbing her, begging for entry - begging to go beyond the flesh.

He had planned to tease her and to take it slow, but the urge was too strong for him. He let out a lust-filled grunt and pushed himself roughly inside of her.

A euphoric moan escaped her lips but was silenced by the tightening belt. Her mind seemed to go out of control. Consciously she knew she was tied up against the wall of a dress shop, with a belt around her neck and being fucked by Mister J. Still, what she saw was different. Maybe it was a vision or a hallucination because of oxygen deprivation, but there was Arkham Asylum.

She could see the dimly lit solitary confinement room – the hole as it was known. The Joker was ravaging her on the old cot. He was penetrating her, holding her down, bringing her to ecstasy over and over again. The guards outside were yelling, telling him to stop while they tried to get the door open. They must've thought he was hurting her – taking her without permission. They were silenced when she got on top of Mister J and began riding him.

"More," she called out in a whisper. She looked around almost surprised she was in the dress shop.

The Joker lifted her body to reposition himself and gave her his full length. He let out a possessive groan of pleasure. She could feel herself twitch against his pulsating cock.

She looked him in his eyes, "Yes, yes, yes," she moved her waist in circular motion not caring that the belt was chafing her neck and growing tighter. Live – die – she didn't care. She just needed to could get there. She craved the sensation -and she was so close. This was it. Her climax surpassed euphoria. It felt as if it were bigger and brighter than heaven itself –an indescribable sexual utopia. It rocked her so deeply that as she trembled, the hook that had been holding her arms up broke.

The Joker's last thrust brought her there again. He let his orgasm spill over her as he let go of the belt. She lowered her legs to the floor, but didn't move. He kissed her shoulder lightly and took the belt off of her neck. He then untied her hands and rubbed her wrists.

Both were out of breath and were silent for a few moments. She sat on the bench to catch her breath. "You definitely know how to treat a lady," she said relaxing against the wall. "That was amazing."

"The games are endless," he straightened out his shirt, buttoned it and threw on his jacket. "Get dressed and meet us in the van in 5." He walked over and kissed her. "People are going to drop dead when they see you."

"And if not, we can help them." She tapped his gun and they both laughed aloud.

"You are a fun one"

He turned around and left while she grabbed new stockings and a brand new pair of panties. She looked over at Christine's dead body and shrugged her shoulders. "She won't mind." She grabbed a shopping back and threw about 20 pairs of panties and a dozen sets of stockings. "With Mister J, a lady needs to be prepared."

She redressed and was about to leave when the belts caught her eye. "Why yes, I do want the home version." She tossed them in the bag and ran out with a minute to spare.

CHAPTER 04

The Joker helped Harley in the van. He sat behind her and pulled her close.

"You ready for tonight. It's going to be unlike anything you've ever seen."

"Oh good, because things have been so boring lately." Harley pretended to yawn and then they both laughed. "Why is North driving like an old lady?"

"Tell him to drive faster." The Joker ran his fingers against her thigh.

"Hey North, speed it up!" Harley called out.

The bulky, tattooed clown looked as though he was going to say something but his eyes caught The Joker's glimpse in the mirror and thought better of it. "You got it." He hit the pedal to the medal and the rest of the guys fell on one another. The Joker held Harley still as they cracked up at the crew.

"Better, pumpkin?"

"Much, Mister J. I can't wait to get to the Waldorf. I want all of Gotham to see me – to really see me."

"What do you want them to see?"

"Me with you. I want them to see that I'm not a hostage. I'm not a victim and I'm not some decoration."

North sort of chuckled at that.

The Joker raised his gun but Harley pushed it back down. "May I?" Harley asked

"Okay, do your thing." He extended his hand.

Harley walked to the front of the van and tapped Chuckles on the shoulder. "I need to sit here and talk to North."

Chuckles nodded, got up and moved out of her way. He sat in the back, while Harley sat in the passenger seat.

"So North, share your thoughts with the whole class. What was so funny?"

North didn't take his eyes off the road. "Nothing Miss Quinn. Forget it."

"I can't. I have a – what do they call it - a photographic memory; especially if someone is being a dick. So, man up, tell me. What did you mean?"

"Why so the boss can shoot me? I know Mister J. I say one word to you, I'm a dead man."

"You are aware that you have two bosses. Mister J and me."

"Sure…whatever." North shook his head in irritation.

"Okay, now you're pissing me off." Harley grabbed a switchblade and held it to his neck. He went to pull over, but Harley ordered otherwise. "I'm not gonna be late because you want to be some goddamn drama queen. If you can't drive, I'll get Chuckles back up here."

"I was driving fine until you came up here."

"No, you were acting like a little bitch and you still are. If you have something to say, say it."

"Fine. I didn't sign up for the Circus to have some chick order me around. I've been working for Mister J for 15 years. When he was in the pen, I ran things. Now, you come in and want a piece of it because you're fucking the boss?"

"You forget, it was my family who had the cash that pays your ass. I'm the one who helped Mister J break out of Arkham. I don't sit on the sidelines. I carry my weight."

"Yeah, but then whenever things don't go your way, you cry and the boss knocks someone off."

"You talking about Juggles?" She sat back down but kept the knife out.

"Yeah, I'm talking about Juggles. Juggles was an asset. I trusted him to have my back when shit went down with the cops."

By this time the Joker was leaning against Harley's seat. She looked over her shoulder and smiled. "I'm good. I got this." She said confidently. "Juggles tried to rape me! That's why he's dead – and I'm the one who killed him."

"Juggles worked with us for a decade. He was dedicated, but then, you come here distracting all the guys and you play Mister J to make him jealous. The end result is we get fucked

"Let's end this now, North – because you're writing your death certificate and you don't even know it. I am your boss. The only reason you're still alive right now is because you're of some value to me, but if you push too hard, I'll slit your throat, jump in the driver's seat and make it to Waldorf all in less than 10 minutes. And if anyone feels distracted by me, please let me know because I'm more than willing to manually castrate them to avoid any confusion in the future. I want you on this team, but that's up to you. So, you tell me, what time is it?"

"Right on time, boss." North forced a smile. "I'm sorry okay. I just don't like people being in charge of my life who I don't know."

"Understandable," Harley nodded. "but all you need to know is that I will kill anyone who comes after you boys. I will stand right in the line of fire to make sure you guys are safe and most importantly to make sure Mister J always comes out on top. That's my mission. I'm not some idiot. I have a Doctorate, a PhD, I was Alpha Epsilon Lamda, and had a 4.0 GPA. I learned to shoot by the time I was 7. That was my family time. My dad would take us to the Gotham gun range. I've succeeded at everything I've ever done – and I was admittedly broken when Mister J came into my life, but he reminded me who I was and what I could do. Don't underestimate me because I'm a woman. I have a 167 IQ and killer intuition. Fuck with me and you'll die. Stick by me, and you'll be a wealthy wealthy man."

"That's my girl," The Joker smiled and took her hand. "Chuckles go back up front." Harley sat with her back against the Joker's chest.

"You did good," he said softly. "If he fucks up again though, he's dead."

"Yes, yes he is." She turned her lips and kissed The Joker hotly as they pulled into the Waldorf. "Now, let's rock-n-roll."

The Joker had 8 more henchmen meeting them. He was happy to see that not only were they all on time, but that they had their gear, were in their places and were ready to fly through the windows on rope when signaled. One had brought his Lamborghini and it was still in perfect shape.

Harley fixed her lipstick and then tossed it in her purse aside her pistol and two knives. She then grabbed an AK-47, loaded it and cocked it. The Joker was loading up when he looked over at her. She was standing like a pro – a sexy pro. His mind replayed the intense encounter at the dress shop. He walked over and kissed her hard. "Purr for me, kitten."

She licked her lips and then rolled her tongue.

"Again," he said when she stopped. Once again she complied. He licked her ear and ran his hand around her waist. "We're going to own the world." The magnitude of his power excited her. She wasn't nervous or afraid, but fired up and aroused by the passion of his words.

The men held back as The Joker and Harley walked in. The maître d stepped back upon seeing the assault weapons. "STOP right there!" He yelled when Harley shot him dead. "I always hated that guy. He'd ogle me as soon as my dad left the room."

The Joker laughed and led her to the main hall. Chuckles and North blocked the front exit and Bozo and Happy took the other.

On stage was a band singing UP & UP. There was a sign above them that said PLAYCOLD.

"A Coldplay tribute band called PlayCold, really? People fucking suck." Harley was disgusted.

The Joker smiled and then took his machine gun. He shot the lead singer and then turned the gun on the rest of the band. Harley watched him in action. He looked like a gangster like the original SCARFACE from 1932.

'Mister J is classy, sexy and all mine' she thought to herself.

When they were all dead, the Joker turned to her. "That's better."

"Yeah it is. Thanks, puddin." Harley smiled and then shot bullets through the ceiling.

The guests were all in black-tie and formal wear. When Harley looked them over she thought back to her engagement party and how no one spoke up for her. She hated them all.

She laughed aloud when the henchmen came in through the windows and scared the Gotham elite to death. They froze. The men wore black and had masks covering their faces. They each had military style weaponry and surrounded the scared bunch. They began patting down each person, grabbing cellphones, purses, wallets and jewelry. That was their payday for pulling this heist off.

The Joker walked on stage and helped Harley up. He took the mic, "Your entertainment for the evening has changed due to the unforeseen death of the band. Now let's take a moment of silence and remember them." Harley bowed her head in faux sympathy as the Joker immediately continued, "and that's enough."

"God, you're fucking awesome." Quinn laughed hysterically.

"Whoa, I think that's Dr. Quinzel!" A voice echoed through the audience.

"Who said that?" Harley put one hand on her hip while the other held her gun. "I want to know who said that?"

Dr. Jeremiah Arkham stepped forward. "I did Harleen. Everyone has been so worried about you."

"I'm sure," she rolled her eyes. "Jeremiah you could care less. You only got your job because your uncle opened Arkham and you only hired me because my dad bribed you to. You could care less about anyone but yourself. You surely don't care about the patients of Arkham."

"Now that's not true! I've worked very hard ….."

"to become rich and to pay Mayor Grange to look the other way when we fail the inspections and have code violations."

"Harleen…"

"Do not call me Harleen. The name is Harley Quinn!"

"Dr. Quinzel, what has happened to you? You are going through some sort of mental breakdown. The Joker is a dangerous and unstable criminal. He killed your father. Do you have Stockholm Syndrome?"

"No, I have Go Fuck Yourself syndrome: AND why does everyone think Mister J killed my dad. I did. I killed him and I killed that skank bitch Alicia." She took out her pistol and shot him dead.

The Joker laughed aloud. "Oh Harl- you become more fun by the day. And you were born to be a sniper.

She curtsied, winked at him and then turned back to the crowd. "Anyone else want to diagnose me or insult Mister J?"

No one said anything so the Joker sighed. "You guys aren't any fun. How is Harley going to perfect her target practice if you guys don't play? Well – if you all are going to be such cowards; I guess we should start the main attraction. Harley-girl, can you get a chair for me and something strong to tie knots with."

"You got it, boss!" She said and did a backflip off the stage never letting go of her gun, just because she could.

"Gymnastics," she said to Gotham's elite who were visibly flabbergasted.

"Mary Lou Retton had nothing on you, babe." The Joker yelled as Harley grabbed a chair.

"You say things like that Mister J, we're gonna have to take a break." She ran her hand over her chest and purred seductively.

"We'll play later, kitten. Trust me, tonight is going to be all kinds of fireworks."

"Yum, can't wait," Harley went into her purse and took out a spool of nylon rope. She waved it at the Joker. "I grabbed it at the house."

"Always such a prepared girl." The Joker admired. "Purr for me, kitten."

She wheeled the chair and the rope to the mayor while looking at the Joker and purring.

"Marion Grange, COME ON DOWN!" The Joker called out as Harley yanked the short stout women and pulled her into the chair. She tied her up without leaving her any room to squirm.

"You heard Mister J. You're the first contestant on his game show."

"What game show? What in God's name are you talking about?"

"You'll see. Take her away boys." Harley motioned for the henchmen to pick her up and put her on stage. "I always wanted to say that."

She jumped back on stage and walked over to The Joker. "Did I do a good job, boss?" She ran her finger down his chest.

"You did really good," He grabbed her hard by the hair and backed her against the wall. They were still on stage in full view of the crowd, but their eyes were only on each other.

"Make sure no one tries anything. Kill anyone who moves." The Joker ordered the men who nodded.

"You know Mister J; I only aim to please you."

He put his hands against the wall and leaned into her. She lifted her dress enough to widen her legs and feel him against her sex. She placed her hands delicately on his neck. Bringing herself to her tiptoes and then slowly down to her tiptoes and slowly down, she rubbed herself against him. "God, I want you to fuck me."

He lowered his hands underneath her dress and rested them on her rear. He parted her mouth with his demanding tongue as he teased the inside of her mouth. His lips fell to her neck. He broke the skin with his teeth and then licked the blood. "Rougher" she said running her leg up and down his.

He caressed her face and then slapped it hard.

"More-please," she begged.

He hit her again, hard. Her body shook and she put her hand inside her tights and on her sex.

The Joker glanced over at Marion and then looked back over at Harley with a wicked victorious smile, "you want to give the mayor a show? After all, it is her party. She's trying to raise money and what sells more than sex? Do you want that?"

"I want you," Harley's lust overpowered every thought. "I don't care who watches. I just want you inside of me." She rubbed herself faster until The Joker pulled her hand away.

He backed away for a moment. "Take your dress off for daddy."

She lifted it over her head and kicked it aside. She stood before him in a bra, panties and fishnets.

"Take off your stockings,"

She pulled them down.

He took his jacket and bowtie off and tossed them on the floor. "Come here. Take off my shirt."

"Yes sir," she walked over and unbuttoned it. As soon as she saw his tattoos, she couldn't help herself. Her mouth fell on them. She licked his chest and stomach. She pushed his shirt off and had both hands on his shoulders nearly climbing on top of him.

He wrapped one arm tightly around her naked waist and kissed her hotly. "You want it?"

"Yes, please daddy. Give it to me." She ran her hand on his hardness. A groan of pleasure escaped his lips. He slapped her hard in the face and then harder on the rear. "God yes," she said nearly dripping wet.

In the background, the entire town was gasping and yelling and jeering, but The Joker and Harley were unfazed. Harley began unfastening his pants, when he pushed her away. He took a step back and with his eyes burning through her soul, he took a deep breath.

"Not until I say"

"Sorry daddy,"

"Take off your bra, for daddy"

She unclasped it and stripped it off of her.

"Your panties, remove them."

She did.

"Are you wet?"

"Yes," was all she could get out practically coming right there.

"Show daddy what you do when you're wet"

She ran her hand against her and began penetrating herself with her fingers. He walked behind her and ran his hands possessively over her body. He lifted her with one hand and brought her in front of the mayor. Marion tried to divert her eyes anywhere else, but she couldn't help but glance at the naked body in front of her.

"I bet you wish you looked this good," he said to the mayor. "Is that why you're such a cunt? You know that a woman like Harley is better than you in every way." He placed his hand on top of hers and stroked her. She ran her wetness against his fingers and rotated her body as orgasmic sensations became close enough to touch.

"Call her a cunt," The Joker teased Harley's pussy silently threatening to stop touching her.

Harley opened her eyes. "You're a jealous cunt." She let out a carnal moan. "You wish you had my body and you wish you had Mister J. You wish you had his cock."

"Jealous?" Marion yelled trying to get Harley's attention. "He hits you!"

"Yes he does." Harley grew even more aroused at the thought. She quickened her motions not caring about anything but getting there.

"For God sakes, you are a doctor! This maniac treats you like a whore."

Harley held his hand and moved back and forth as he penetrated her. "As long as he keeps fucking me, I'll be his whore – I'll be his slut -I'll be his sex kitten – I'll be whatever he wants."

He turned her around and with his hand on her back guided her to the floor. "Daddy wants to play now," he said with a dark wanton lust that nearly pushed her over the edge. "Take my cock out." She was beneath him, his waist inches away from her mouth.

"Yes sir," she unzipped his pants, and lowering his boxes took him out. She let out an immodest gasp of pure ecstasy.

"Anything you want to do; you have to ask me. You have to beg me, kitten."

She licked her lips and instinctively went to take him into her mouth. He slapped her hard across the face. The erotic excitement pushed her over the edge as her body shook.

"Beg me." He held his long cock in his hand and ran it across her lips.

"Please Mister J. I want to taste you. I want to lick you. I want to make you come in my mouth. I need it."

A grunt escaped his lips. "Good girl, take it all."

Another lustful tremor hit her. "Thank you,"

She licked his tip and moved her mouth up and down on the shaft. Her fingers danced on his balls. She moved her lips to them and took one and then the other suckling them. She could feel him near the edge but before he came he pushed her hard to the ground.

"The mayor called you my whore." He grabbed her legs and wrapped them around his waist.

"I don't care. I'd rather be your whore than anyone else's wife."

He slammed into her hard. "You're not my whore," he whispered driving into her again and again. "You're – fuck – you're my babe."

"Oh God," she matched his movements and pushed back against him. She rolled him over and impaled herself onto him. "You're my master – my boss -my very own sex GOD!" She rode him and climaxed hard. He grabbed hold of her waist and pierced her clit. "You're…. IT! Oh fucking Yes!" She came again as her nails dug into his chest. "You're my world."

He lifted her up and was on top of her again. He began fucking her selfishly. He held her down and positioned himself at her center. He penetrated her and let out gasps of gratification. "Everyone knows your mine now. Say it! Say it!"

"I'm yours. My body is yours. You can do whatever you want to me. I'm your sex toy." She said widening her legs as he shoved himself in over and over.

"Mine....my mouth," He kissed her hard. "My tits," he caressed them roughly and bit down. She panted like a cat in heat. "My pussy," He placed his hands on her thighs and bearing down drove himself into her.

He inhaled and heaved trying to catch his breath. "You want me to come in your mouth?" He asked still pumping inside of her.

"YES, yes, I want it. Please face fuck me."

He pulled out and knelt. He forcefully grabbed her up and pushed her head. She took him and sucked him hungrily. She licked him and practically gagged at his length and width. Intent on giving him the best blowjob she used her saliva to make his dick nice and wet. She teased the underside of his cock with her tongue. She swirled it around him as he jerked and groaned.

"That's a good girl. Make daddy come." He grunted and thrust harder.

She ran her hand over his balls and then licked them while looking into his eyes.

"Such a good sex toy." He said moving her head back on his cock. He was pulsating and so close. She ran her hands up and down his shaft while she worked the tip and ridge. She flicked her tongue against him.

She took his cock and put it in-between her breasts and moved them up and down. "You like that daddy?"

He let out a deep animalistic groan. "I'm gonna come. Fucking yeah, I'm gonna come. Put me in your mouth, now. I need to come in your mouth."

She gladly obliged as he pushed hard into her throat and spilled his seed.

"FUCK," he called out as he pulled himself out of her mouth. He watched her lick her lips after swallowing him.

She threw her dress back on but left the rest of the clothing. He left his shirt off and straightened out his pants. He then picked a machine gun off the stage floor. He looked at the mayor and shot her in the leg.

"Nobody calls my babe a whore," his tone was dark. He then shot her other leg as Marion screamed out in pain.

"Mister J, it appears we have company."

The Joker turned his head to see Batman flying through the window.

"Batsy, Batsy, Batsy – here to save the day, but you're a bit too late. Harley, my dear, kill the mayor." The Joker kept his gun on Batman while Harley let out an excited gasp and turned to the mayor. She took her hunting knife out.

"This is the knife I killed my father with. It's kind of special to me. It's only fitting that you die with it. My dad was a corrupt cop. You're a corrupt mayor." Within seconds she was on top of the mayor stabbing her. "In and turn, in and turn," she chanted to The Joker's delight.

"Isn't she a spitfire?" He asked Batman.

"Get off of her!" He was too late. The mayor was dead and Harley was covered in blood. "What is wrong with you?" Batman tried to move forward but the Joker kept his gun on him.

"Me? I'm not the one who is dressed like a bat and talking like a 13 year old boy trying to sound like a man. You have problems! Mister J and I have solutions. That's the difference. You sit back and watch all the insanity that these people cause and you do nothing! Mister J changes the world."

"For the worse! He kills people!"

"So, everyone dies. Life is a big fucking joke. You of all people should get that. I mean look at you. I do have a question for you, Batsy. I always wondered. What do you wear on Halloween? Do you wear something over your bat suit?"

Batman just stared at her so she shrugged and rolled her eyes. "but I have problems….."

The Joker laughed aloud. "Well, Batsy it's been fun, but Miss Quinn and I have more parties to crash. Bye bye." He grabbed Harley and disappeared through the back of the stage and the exit as the henchmen held Batman off.

His pink Lamborghini was waiting outside. He held the door for Harley and he jumped in the driver seat. "Let's go home." He said driving as fast as the car would go.

She moved into his arms and kissed his neck. "Tonight was amazing."

"Tomorrow, my dear, will be even better. Tomorrow we kill Batman."

Harley smiled and nuzzled closer. "I can't wait to hear your plan."

"I'm sure you can think of a few ways to get it out of me." He placed his hand around her waist and pulled her close.

She rubbed his thigh and then moved her hand to his cock. She leaned back and began rubbing him through his pants. He was hard as a rock and ready to play.

"Insatiable sex kitten. Purr for me."

She purred and placed her hand inside of his pants. "I love the way you feel."

"Yeah, I love when you beg me to fuck you. I love when you need it so much that you'll let me put anything inside of you."

He arrived at his secret layer and pulled into the hidden garage.

"You want to play a game?"

"Yes," she whispered and took off her dress. Naked in front of him she opened her legs to expose herself. She ran her hand up and down. "You make me so wet."

"Get out of the car," he ordered. She did. Standing in the garage she waited for him to get out and come around. HE took her by the hand and brought her to the front of the car. "Come on, jump up."

She did as she was told.

"Show me your pussy."

She opened herself to him.

"Now lean back."

She did. She was lying on the car spread eagle.

He grabbed a clean rag and put it on her as a blindfold.

"Don't touch yourself and stay that way."

He disappeared behind her. She heard him open something and moving things around. Part of her wanted to ask what he was doing, but she knew he hated questions. After a few moments, he returned and placed objects that felt metal on the car.

"Harley-girl, are you ready for our game?"

"Yes Mister J"

She suddenly felt an object running against her. She felt herself dripping. It was then inside of her.

"you like that?"

She placed her hand above her and pushed up on the object.

"You like that?" he repeated piercing her.

"YES, YES," she moaned rocking against it. Then it was out of her.

"any guesses what that was?"

"A screwdriver?" she asked.

"One point for Harley."

Next there was a long piece of wood running up and down. She could feel the width against her. She felt a cold piece of metal on the top. "Put it inside of me. Please daddy." She was bouncing against it.

He shoved it in and she cried out in ecstasy.

"That's it baby. Fuck it."

She closed her legs on it and rocked back and forth. She was right there when he withdrew it.

"What was that Harley?"

"A hammer?" she said out of breath wanting to lower her hand, but knowing that was against the rules.

It took Mister J a few moments to get the next object ready. She heard a click and then what sounded like a grinder.

He placed it on her center. The object was spinning. It was cloth and round and it was so close to going inside of her. She pushed herself up and then groaned as it was in her.

"That's it. Right there." She fucked it hard. "MISTER J…oh god."

He shut it off and pulled it out once again right as her body was responding. Her body had tightened against it and was twitching, begging to reach that point.

Next, it was his body on top of her. She felt his hardness and yearned for it.

"Do you know what that last one was?" He whispered as he lifted her waist and pushed himself inside of her.

"A drill with something attached." She placed her arm around him and matched his rhythm.

"I'll give you a half a point. It was a paint roller cover attached. You got it all wet." He said bringing it to her lips. "Lick it for daddy."

"Oh God," she licked it.

He put it down and picked up the hammer.

"you like fucking a hammer?" He asked driving himself even harder. "Put it in your mouth. Suck on it. I want to watch you do it."

She did. She acted as though it was his cock and sucked it for him. Blindfolded, with him inside of her, was too much. The throes of passion erupted inside of her. She tightened herself around him and her entire body shook.

"That's it. Such a good girl." He threw the hammer on the floor, kissed her hard and slammed into her a few more times. He ripped off the blindfold and stared at her.

She circled his waist with her legs and matched every movement.

"You're amazing. You're my God" She called out.

He came hard in her and held her as his body throbbed and vibrated in her.

When he finally sat up and got off the car he looked up at her. "We're good together."

She saw the unmistakable look in his eyes. She smiled. "I love you too."

He tilted his head from side to side and then let out a smirk. "Let's go inside."

"Yes sir" she said hopping off the car and putting her dress on.

CHAPTER 05

The Joker, outstretched on his bed awaited Harley. He had his pants unbuckled and his shirt unbuttoned. He stared at his black ceiling with glow-in-the-dark stickers that said "HA HA" all over them. He flicked the lamp by his bed on and off to look at the stickers. He finally settled down with the light on and glanced at his cell phone to see what time it was.

'Today was a great!' he thought to himself. He thought about Harley stabbing the Mayor in front of Batman; Batsy standing there helpless and unable to stop it. He thought of her stabbing Marion over and over again as blood spattered; and Harley loved it. 'That's my girl,' his cock hardened.

"Harley-girl, why are you keeping daddy waiting? Get in here."

"I'll be there in one second. I have a surprise for you."

"I'm not a patient man so it better be worth it, pumpkin."

She arrived by his last syllable. She stood in a short red sequence nightie that was tight around the chest and covered only the top of her thighs. She had bright red lipstick and her hair in tightened perfect ponytails. She leaned against the door holding a piece of paper in her hand.

"Do you like me in this?" She posed with her chin on her shoulder, staring at him, with her chest nearly exposed.

"Come over and find out," he said licking his lips and sending fiery glares of enticement her way.

She saw his member at full attention. She let out a swooning sound of excitement. "Don't you want to know about my surprise," she waved the paper in the air and then walked over and crawled on the bed. She draped half her body on his and ran her leg against his sex.

She handed him the paper. "I found this in my files. I knew I had it somewhere, but I thought we could use it on Batsy – really screw with him. Then we kill him. Stabb-ie, Stabb-ie, Stabb-ie" she said in between kissing his chest and running her hands up and down his tats. "You're so sexy."

He read while enjoying the sensation of having Harley on his body. He adjusted himself and wrapped his free arm around her to feel her even closer.

"This is interesting..." he said as he ran his hand underneath her nightie and on her naked rear. He grabbed it and slapped it.

"I thought you might like it," Harley was instinctively moving against his cock begging for some fun. She let out a small hungry moan.

"What's the plan?" He lowered his lips to her neck and bit thru the skin making her let out a moan of pure need.

"Well Mister J, I learned about this whole MK Ultra stuff from this Arkham inmate The Mad Hatter. He was a geeky little guy who kind of had a thing for me. I was NOT interested in the least but during one of our sessions, he mentioned MK Ultra. It was a mixture of drugs and chemicals that the government used to make the perfect soldier. They would give them orders to kill people and stuff and they would do it. Mad Hatter used it to keep a girlfriend of his until Batsie ruined it. So, you had all the chemicals to make this stuff…"

"Of course I do, pumpkin. You don't think you're dealing with an amateur do you?"

"Never Mister J. I'm in awe of you. I mean you're the Clown Prince of Gotham and - oh God" As he pushed against her she quivered, "you have the biggest cock I've ever seen." Her hands tugged his pants and boxers down. She sat up and on top of him, widening her legs and positioning herself so he was inside of her.

"Hungry little kitten, purr for daddy." He said now holding the paper so tight in his hand it nearly ripped.

She purred as she rode him up-and-down, like a manual seesaw from heaven. She grasped onto his shirt as she quickened her pace.

"Okay, so tell me what we do to Batsy…" he said knowing her ruse already, but wanting to give her the glory - and to make her speak while she reached her apex.

"Fuck – um – ok Mister J – we stick him with a needle of this stuff – and we – oh my God…." She shook and her body tightened on him.

"Go on." The Joker dropped the paper and leaned back enjoying the view of her tits popping out of her nightie as she bounced up and down. The poor thing tried to stay focused but his cock knew her too well and found the spot like a pro every time. "Harley- darling, what's next."

Damn, he's so arrogant. He knows…fuck…..he knows what he's doing to me. He's so fucking amazing.

Her thoughts scrambled as she tried to finish."Okay, okay, Mister J so we make Batsy kill a bunch of people and then he's a wanted man and thrown in Arkham."

"Great plan, dollface. I'm in." Before she knew what he was doing, he flipped her over and tore her nightie off. "It's a nice little thing, but I like my girl naked." He ran his tongue on her breast as she pushed forward giving him full access. "You know what I like about you."

She shook her head no and tried to push against him, but he pinned her down. He teased her with his cock as she panted in need.

"I like that you chose to fuck the serpent. Do you know what I'm talking about?"

"No, Mister J, but just please – please fuck me."

He was piercing her and damn - she needed it so bad. She could feel his body begging to come in and hers was holding up the welcome sign. The Joker refused to give into it. "Come on baby, please. Please, I'll do anything." Her voice was cracking as she grew desperate.

"Poor insatiable baby," he lowered his mouth and sucked on her hard nipple. It was almost painful within the boundaries of pleasure. "You see, in the Bible," he pushed against her but still didn't enter.

She cried out in pain.

"Now listen, Harley."

"I am. I swear. I'm listening daddy." She said as her body jerked up. He put all his weight onto her so she couldn't move.

"Stay still angel, Daddy's in control."

"Yes sir," she just wanted him to say what he was going to say so she could feel him inside of her.

"Well, in the Bible the first two people on earth were Adam and Eve – and see God told Eve she couldn't eat an apple from a tree, but when the serpent arrived he told her to take a bite." He thrust and allowed his tip to enter.

"Oh God, yes, Mister J, I'm listening."

"You my dear, ate the whole apple and then ran off and fucked the serpent. You're on the left-hand side with the devil and this is hell - it's our playground. And now my sweet sexy kitten, I think it's time I punish you." His tone was dark and frightening. Any other girl would want out, but not her.

"Punish me, daddy." She purred for him. "I was given a get-out-of-hell-free card and I set it on fire. I want to be here and I want to be punished."

He lightened his grip and allowed her to circle around his cock. He released her arms and allowed her to move her legs. "Okay, one fun little fuck, and then it's time for your penance."

"Yes, Yes, please fuck me." Her nails were clawing at him and her legs wrapped tightly around opening herself. "I'm dripping baby."

He kissed her hard, his tongue owned her mouth. He groaned against her trembling lips as he entered her fast and deep. "That's the way my baby likes it, isn't it. Huh, you like it raw….you like it rough….just like daddy."

He took his hand and hit her straight across the face.

"Yes, more. More. Your fucking cock is incredible, baby – it's oh god – it's gonna tear thru me. I live for this. I need this all the time. I want you to live inside of me. Fuck…baby YES."

He held onto the headboard and rammed into her knowing he was tearing her, knowing he was hurting her in the way she needed to be hurt. "You like it when daddy comes, don't you. Little sex toy, needs it."

She climaxed. Tremors ran through her body as she clutched on to him. "I'm your sex toy. Come in me like I'm your sex toy. Fill me baby."

"That's tempting, but it's not fair to your beautiful little mouth. Open wide, daddy's about to gag the fuck out of you."

"Do it...I want it."

He pinned her down, once more and positioned himself so his cock was against her mouth. He held onto the headboard. He ran his cock, her wetness, and precum against her lips. "Baby, I'm gonna fuck you til your lips split open."

"Oh God yes," she licked her lips.

"Open your mouth," She widened her mouth as much as she could. He used the headboard as leverage and pushed himself so far down her throat he could feel her tonsils. She immediately started gagging but he didn't stop. It made it more intense.

"My little fucking sex toy want her daddy to cum in her mouth. You want to taste it. You want to feel me explode. Feel this baby." He shoved himself harder and saw blood trickle from her lips. Still, she ran her tongue around his shaft and tried her best to keep up with his pace.

He began moving in a circular motion holding her head against him the whole time. "You're just a clit, baby. Your mouth, your tits, your beautiful hair, every part of you – I can cum on. Every part of you is just a pussy in disguise. OH yeah, baby, that's what I'm gonna do. You're gonna sleep in my cum. Keep your mouth open. I want you to catch as much as you can. " He pulled out of her, shoved her down on the bed and spilled his seed everywhere. His release could be heard by anyone in a country mile. She moved her head, lapping every drop she could up.

He stared at her, "beautiful…so fucking beautiful."

Small after-shocks surged through her as she ran her fingers across her body and then sucked on them trying to get every taste she could.

"Are you ready," he ran his hand across her face lightly. "It's time for your punishment."

She sat up and a look of pure anticipation took over her face. "Punish me, daddy!"

He got up, got dressed and walked over to the closet. "Don't put on any clothes, cupcake. Get on the floor. Lie on your back with both your arms and both legs spread as far apart as you can. I'll re-position you when I get all the toys ready."

She rose from the bed and tried to take a look into his closet.

"No peeking sweetheart, it ruins the surprise!"

"Yes sir," She did as she was told and got on the floor.

She heard him throw some large objects on the bed. He walked over to her and sat down. He gently ran his hand against her skin. "What happens next is very …let's say...intense. Anyone with any sensibilities would run for the hills. You could still say that I brainwashed you, that you were just a victim yourself, and let's face it Harley-girl, you're hot enough to go free – and I wouldn't kill you. I wouldn't even hurt you. So, it's your choice - what's you're pleasure – pure sweet Adam and Eden - a life of harmony - boring harmony, but harmony…" he pointed toward the door offering her the life she used to know and the Gotham before the insanity -"OR you could choose me, the serpent who intends to steal your soul only to use it and abuse it – to bring you down to the darkest and most depraved places - to my level. I'll get you so messed up that you'll lust over all the bad things you were warned about, the things that make most people cringe." His fingers were now at her lips. "What do you want, kitten?"

There was no pause – no hesitation – not even a moment when she considered the options. She knew the answer. She opened her mouth, rolled her tongue, and purred for him.

He lowered his mouth to hers. She licked and bit his lips. She let her tongue wander into his mouth – owning it – knowing this was the last bit of control she'd have for a while.

He laughed aloud, "you have moxie, balls of steel and a hot little body that I'll never get sick of ravaging. Now, if you want to end this little game, you gotta tell me. The way you tell me is to say, I Want Eden."

"You will never hear those words come out of my mouth. Mister J, it's always you."

He let out a satisfied animalistic groan. "I was hoping you'd say that. Let's get started."

He brought over a large thick wooden plank with three holes. It stood about three feet on the ground. "This my dear is REAL oak – I had it made for you – your measurements – it should fit perfectly. The ones they sell in the store, simply won't do. They are just not made for the type of fun we'll be having. Put your hands through the two holes furthest apart and head through the other one. You'll have to be on your knees."

"That's a position I'm very familiar with." She rose to her knees and did as she was told.

"Oh pumpkin, you already broke the rules – and before I even had a chance to go over them. No talking unless I ask you a question." He took out a switchblade from his pocket and opened it. It was small but it was sharp.

He knelt behind her and ran it against her body, scraping her but not cutting her. In a blackened, eerie tone he began to sing.

Eeny, meeny, miny, moe,

Catch a tiger by the toe.

If he hollers, let him go,

Eeny, meeny, miny, moe.

When he stopped singing he was right in between her legs. "Now open your legs but don't fall. Show me those gymnast skills, Miss Quinn."

She widened her legs for him. He took this knife and once again sang the last lyric, "moe…" He pushed the knife against her, drawing a small amount of blood.

Rather than react in pain, she became aroused. "Oh Mister J"

He wanted to bring down the other toys. He wanted to punish her more, but he couldn't. He needed her. His body longed for her.

He rose to his feet, went over to his music selection. He decided on a song that he hadn't heard for a while but damn it fit now. It was CLOSER by NIN (Nine Inch Nails).

The song began. The music was so loud that even if she said something, he couldn't hear. He slowly, menacingly walked toward her. He took off his belt and unbuttoned his pants.

You let me violate you

You let me desecrate you

You let me penetrate you

You let me complicate you

He hit her hard with the leather belt and then threw it on the floor. He knelt behind her and in a domineering pompous way, rubbed his erection right in the middle on her rear. His hands raked over her breasts, ran down her stomach and danced against her wet center.

Help me, I broke apart my insides

Help me, I've got no soul to sell

Help me, the only thing that works for me

Help me get away from myself

He glanced at a mirror and saw her staring at him. She licked her lips and he could see her purr. 'Such a good girl. I want to be inside this good girl. I want this good girl to be grinding her ass on my cock. I'm gonna take everything in her – it's mine.' His own thoughts and the soundtrack behind him along with the view of Harley made him crazy. He pulled off his pants in a rush, licked his hands and used his saliva to make it a little easier on her. After all, I don't want to kill her.

I want to fuck you like an animal

I want to feel you from the inside

I want to fuck you like an animal

My whole existence is flawed

You get me closer to god

He firmly grabbed her waist and with a thrust was in her from behind. He watched her face in the mirror and as aroused as she was, he knew this was the first time anyone had fucked her this way – in this place. Words escaped his lips despite being drowned out by music.

"Fucking tight, - so fucking tight, baby. Nobody ever had you like this. Fucking sex toy. I'll take you whatever way I want. I fucking own you. You can't fucking move. You just have to take it. I'm the snake in the garden, the snake inside of you that you can't resist."

Despite being confined, Harley wanted him to have the best of her. She scraped her neck on the wooden plank by trying to push back as far as she could. He was moving quickly. He placed one hand on her back and the other inside of her, penetrating her from the front. She instinctively rode his hand, and he could feel her juices squirting. The orgasm was too much and the flesh on her wrists were bleeding. She saw the blood trickle down her finger and felt the small wounds, but still she moved on him – needing him to have all of her.

You can have my isolation

You can have the hate that it brings

You can have my absence of faith

You can have my everything

Help me, tear down my reason

Help me, it's your sex I can smell

Help me you make me perfect

Help me become somebody else

The Joker stood and brought Harley up with him. He reached with one hand and unclasped the wooden plank – not to let her free, but just so he could fuck her harder. Still inside of her, he brought her to the bed. He pushed her head and chest against the bed, wrapped his hand tighter around her waist and watched as her ass bounced against his cock. In and out – In and out – as those words crossed his mind, In and Turn, In and Turn found their way in. The visual of Harley stabbing her father, Alicia, and Marion danced in his mind.

The pulsations and vibrations of The Joker mixed with that of the blasting music that shook the house was too much for Harley. She came hard and the experience brought tears of euphoric bliss to her eyes.

I want to fuck you like an animal

I want to feel you from the inside

I want to fuck you like an animal

My whole existence is flawed

You get me closer to god

Through every forest, above the trees

Within my stomach, scraped off my knees

I drink the honey inside your hive

You are the reason I stay alive

The song ended and only uncontrollable lustful wanton sounds from the Joker's mouth could be heard. He felt Harley's orgasm as her body shuddered and jerked rapidly. Her insides contracted and clenched down on him in the most satisfying of ways. He took his hand from her legs and grabbed a hold of the comforter. She was a like a rag-doll, being thrown around as he fucked her.

He pulled her up by her hair and held her still with an arm around the stomach. He licked her neck gently as his cock drove into her again and again. Against her naked skin he whispered, "you like being fucked like this? Tell daddy you like it. Tell daddy you're a bad girl. Tell daddy you let the snake come inside of you." He was nearly at his apex, he just needed to hear her voice.

She turned her head and looked into his eyes. "Daddy, I let the snake fuck me. I loved it daddy. That snake makes me wet, daddy." His breath became rapid and her sex was awakened once more. She put her fingers inside of her and rode against both his cock and her hand. "I'm a bad girl. I like being punished. Teach me daddy. I need to know more about the serpent – oh god daddy I love your snake. Fuck me with your snake. OH God, Oh God."

He pushed her on the bed and with one last thrust came. He stayed in her letting every drop fall. After he pulled out he wiped his dick on her rear. He slapped her ass hard, walked over to his side of the bed and slid in.

She rolled over and was still stroking her sex relishing every spasm of ecstasy. "Ohhhh Mister J."

She withdrew her hand and let out one last sexual gasp. They were both spent. They looked at each other and began laughing.

"Hey, you wanna be Mrs. J?" The Joker asked nonchalantly causing Harley to sit right up in the bed. "Don't make a big deal out of it or anything but we're good together – mine as well make sure in the event of an arrest, the cops can't force us to testify against one another."

"Excellent point, Mister J – and I would be honored." She attempted to look nonchalant but she couldn't help but glow….and despite the tough exterior The Joker was showing, he had an ulterior motive too…. He was going to make sure his little sex kitten stayed put. She belonged to him – and maybe, just maybe, he belonged to her too.

CHAPTER 06

The next morning, Harley stumbled out of bed. She could barely walk after all the fun of the previous night. The Joker was still fast asleep in bed so she brushed her teeth, took a hot massaging shower, dried her hair and put it up in her now classic ponytails.

She grabbed a red corset, a black tight skirt, panties, stockings and red heeled boots that cut off at the calf.

She fed Bud and Lou some rare prime-rib and then made the omelets that would make Martha Stewart envious. She fried up some bacon and sliced soft new bread for toast. She made some fresh squeezed orange juice and coffee to boot. She knew The Joker like his jet black with a shot of espresso. Typically, she used sugar and cream, but curiosity got the best of her and she made hers precisely the way Mister J liked it.

She placed it all on a tray, and in one trip without so much a spill, made it back to the room. She put it all down on the table next to her side of the bed. She crawled over to The Joker and cuddled next to him.

"Sweetie Pie, wake-y wake-y"

The Joker opened one eye and then the other. He sat up and looked over her shoulder "What do we have here? I didn't take you for Harley the Homemaker."

"I'm a little of everything." She smirked and handed him his coffee. "Black with a shot of espresso."

"Very observant,"

She brought his plate over and handed it to him with a fork, knife and cloth napkin.

"Complex, Harley-girl."

"It's just an omelet," she said taking a bite of her own.

He laughed aloud for a few moments. "It's not the food or the coffee, girl. It's you – It's Harley Quinn! My creation! My monster. My beautiful atrocity. You're the pitch black sky on a starless night and the heat of the sun on the brightest day of the year. Don't you feel it? It's all over your face and your body – it's in your actions – your reactions – instincts and motivations. It's all of you. Temperament, and choice, nature and nurture, freewill and destiny colliding to make. – you.

"I love the way you talk Mister J. It's eloquent – meaningful. People don't get honesty – brutal honesty y'know. You have the Batmans of the world running around everyone that he's keeping them safer, and they believe it. They believe that this one idiot in spandex and a cape can protect them from all the horrors of the world – not even realizing that they are the true horror. They're the ones that lie to themselves when they look in the mirror – getting facelifts, tummy tucks, bigger tits – bigger asses – and then they lie about it. They spend thousands of dollars on these operations and then swear to God that it's all-natural. They'd run over a little old lady for a dollar when no one was looking. They only have a problem when you're honest about it – and that's what you are – all honesty. You're brutal with a capital B, but you're honest."

"Doris Day, Bonnie Parker, Squeaky Fromme, Lizzie Borden and Harley Quinn. We, pumpkin, are going down in history – and you know what they say about history. It's written by the winners and I don't lose."

"Me neither – not anymore. Not since you."

"And not ever again." He finished his food and put the plate down. He took a sip of the juice. "Not bad, Harley-girl. Not bad at all."

"Thank you," she finished hers and put it aside. "So, Mister J, about this M.K. Ultra biz. How should we start?"

"Patience, doll-face. If we're gonna make Batsy a killer, we can't do it one day after we crash the Waldorf party. We need to give it a few days. Then we act small. We have him commit petty crimes, then bigger gigs, and then a kill of the century – Officer Gordon."

"Oooooh, his best friend – I like that."

"Yeah, that's because you're a bad girl who likes bad things and bad men."

"I don't know about that Mister J. I'm not convinced you're a man."

"Questioning my manhood?" He turned a bit to her and stared.

"Not at all." She ran her hand against his cock. "I know what you have, but that's it. You're more than a man – bigger than it – like Ramesses or Cain."

"So you do know your Bible."

"Yeah, maybe I went to a Catechism class or two. They didn't like me too much."

"Poor baby, why didn't they like you?"

She unzipped her skirt, let it fall off her, crawled on top of him and straddled him. Her boot hung off the side of the bed. "Because I always liked the bad boys. Like Abel was a goodie goodie always showing up his brother so Cain reacted."

"That's right." He ran his hand through her hair as she placed her sex against his. "They kicked you out?"

"Yes, they didn't like me."

"And why is that, pumpkin and don't tell me it's because you had a thing for Judas."

"No, that's not why."

He tore the buttons off her corset and her hands wrapped around it to hold it still.

"Drop it. Don't you know that during confession, there are no secrets – nothing to hide."

She threw the corset to the floor and raised her neck to fully expose herself to him. He ran his hands possessively over them. "Tell me why you were kicked out of church."

"Okay, I 19 and my father thought if I went to this stupid church that I'd be a better person and it would boost his image so the whole family went to this god forsake place. and the president of the church – you know the priest – guy with the collar…"

"I'm familiar – many have condemned me."

She laughed, "we got that in common then. Well, this guy does his whole sermon thing just for us 'teens' and he asks me to stay after session. So, I do and this man of God starts telling me he likes my legs…"

"they are nice, but they're mine." He said tearing into her fishnets.

"Yeah they are, well he went on to say I had a lot of nice things and if I ever wanted to learn how to satisfy my husband and to be a good wife that he could help me with that."

"I haven't killed a priest in a while, wanna do that?"

"Sure, anything with you. It's Father Jordan over at Christ is the King."

"So, tell me how this story ended."

"I kicked him in the nuts, called my dad, Jordan told my dad I through myself at him and he refused, so I was called a slut and never went to church again, so in a way I won."

The Joker picked up his burner cell and texted North. Get me Father Jordan in the Chem Room – 2 hours.

"Jordan will be here in two hours."

Harley laughed aloud and then lowered her mouth to his gently. She kissed him light at first but then intensified the meeting of their lips. She danced her tongue in his mouth and grazed her teeth against his skin.

She could feel him harden against her.

"You're amazing Mister J. I tell you something bad that happened a million years ago and you just bam wipe it clean." She ran her hand down his chest. "I have a favor to ask you."

"and you choose now, Harley-girl to ask. Smart. Tell daddy what you want."

"I want you but I want to take it. I want to be in control. Just this once – unless you like it – then who knows." She unsnapped her panties and tore them off.

"I like those,"

"Is that a yes?" She lowered his boxers and ran her hand up and down his shaft before impaling herself onto him. Before he could answer, she murmured "Fuck yes,"

"Okay princess, just this once. You take care of daddy."

She lowered her lips to his and kissed him, she then moved her mouth to his ear, teasing it with her tongue. "I'll take great care of you, daddy. I promise."

She grabbed two pair of handcuffs off the table next to her. He stared at them for a moment.

"Ooooh, you're serious. Where's the key for those?"

"You're the Joker. You don't need keys."

"Great answer," he extended his hands as she took one and then the other handcuffing his hands to each side of the bedpost.

"Gotta admit, never been on this side before,

"Just lie back and enjoy it.'

She grabbed a lighter and a cigarette out his drawer. She lit it took a puff and then placed it in his mouth. He inhaled and she then put it on an ashtray beside her.

"So Mister J, can I go in the closet and see all the toys?"

"No Harley, those are just for you and they're all surprises."

She faux-pouted for a second but then nodded. "Yes sir," She leaned down against his chest, stretching out her legs past the ends of the bed. Her sex never left his while she moved. She licked his chest and bit him.

"I can improvise with what I see." She gently rolled off of him and as she withdrew he let out a groan.

"You better hurry, or you'll see how quickly I can get out of these things." He banged the handcuffs.

"There is something very hot about you being a willing prisoner." She grabbed a long frayed leaf off one of his plants and then grabbed her hunting knife out of her bag. "Let's play," she proudly showed both of her toys.

"Bring it, doll-face."

She crawled on top of him gripping both toys. She felt him jerk up immediately, instinctively looking for her sex.

"Not yet," she said and then ran her leaf on his body down to his member. He twitched at the sensation. She ran the knife against her own body. She sat up and only slightly scraping her skin ran the knife from her neck to her navel.

"What do you want, Mister J?"

"Fuck, come on get on top of daddy."

"Don't you want to play first."

"You want to play?"

"Yeah, daddy. I want to play." She pushed herself onto him fully, groaned in pleasure and then pulled herself up and out again.

She had a dark look on her eyes, a daring look. She wanted him to break through. With one hard pull the wooden nightstand broke. The handcuffs still hung around his hand but were unattached to anything else.

"You are just a beautiful maniac," she said with her eyes wide and lit as if she just saw a fireworks show.

He was on top of her quickly. He held one leg over his arm and rammed her again and again.

"You like that Harley? You like that? What about this?" He circled himself inside of her. She banged her head against the pillow and her fingers raked his back. She let out noises that were meant to be words but in the throes of passion got lost.

She was already in heaven when he spilled his seed all over her.

He rolled off of her and they both lay out of breath. His phone went off and he looked at the text.

"Darling, it appears you have a friend who has come to save you from my evil clutches."

"What? What are you talking about? Who?"

"A Miss Pamela Isley"

"Poison Ivy….." she said quietly. "She was my patient, my friend at Arkham."

"Ahhhh, well Isley and I rarely see eye to eye but she's broke out of the asylum and came all the way here to say hi, so the least we can do is talk to her."

The Joker showed up in the living room as Harley threw herself together. He had one of his tailored purple suits on and the smile that irritated the hell out of Isley – It was a smile that bragged he was holding all the cards.

She was standing on top of a large plant she created through the power of Green. Long ago, The Joker used the antidote to all of her toxins and he knew she wouldn't try anything on Harley.

The Joker waved off North, grabbed himself a shot of whiskey and then handed a wine glass to Isley. Her red hair flowed down to her shoulders and she wore a green flowered print tie-around dress with a slit up the hip. She stepped down from her vine but kept it wrapped around her like a wedding train.

"Pam- Pamela – Pammie – so good to see you. You were always a Chardonnay gal." The Joker filled the glass, but Pam just put it down without drinking it

"Where is she?"

"She? Who? Listen, this is over a $100 a glass. I'm not going to waste it." He began laughing and drank it himself.

"HARLEEN, Dr. Quinzel! Where is she? What have you done with her?"

"Oh her. I killed her – drowned her in acid."

"You son of a – "She went to strike The Joker when Harley emerged from the room. She was wearing a bright red dress with black diamond shape decorations around it. She had bright red stockings on and high heeled red shoes. Her white face glowed. Her red lipstick shined. She was gorgeous.

"Hey Red," Harley waved. "How'd you find me?"

"Harleen!" Ivy ran over to her and wrapped her arms around her. "What happened?"

"Long story, but first, it's Harley now – Harley Quinn. Mister J picked it out."

Ivy glared at the Joker but then turned back to Quinn. "This clown is bad news. He's an egomaniacal sociopath. Do you know you guys are the talk of the town? Everyone is looking for you – everyone."

"That's so cool!" Harley shot a smile at The Joker who returned it.

"Now, now Pammie, I'm right in the room." Mister J walked over and behind Harley. He intertwined his arms around her waist and pulled her against him. "Be nice."

"You can have this room – this haven of hell. We're going to leave." Ivy tried to grab Harley's hand but Harley was still. "Come on. You can't want to stay with with this…."

"Yes, I can. I do. I love Mister J. He's my soulmate. He's my heart." She used her fingers to make a heart shape.

"Poor Pammie, you just don't have the right equipment for Harley-girl." He leaned into Quinn's backside and ran his fingers down her stomach. "But that doesn't mean you can't play with us."

"You're no good for her! You're using her! I know you are."

"Excuse me for one second, doll-face." The Joker kissed Harley's hand and walked from behind her and to Ivy. "And why do you care? I mean, unless you have a thing for me…" He ran his hand down Ivy's arm and she recoiled.

"I do. It's called disgust. I'm disgusted with you."

"Oh well, then it's Harley. You have a thing for my Harley."

"Yes, friendship. Something you know nothing about." She turned to Harley. "I care about you."

"I care about you too, Red, but Mister J – well, he's just everything."

"Thank you, Harley girl. Now Ivy, this is some predicament. You care about Harl, she cares about me, I care about – me. Now, I'd hate to think you're worried about her. Come here, your good friend is worried about you. Let's show her how you're doing."

Harley began to walk when The Joker raised his hand. "No. No. No. Crawl to daddy."

She got down on all fours and started crawling seductively. Her dress flared with the fan revealing her thong panties.

"You don't have to do this! You're a doctor, a strong woman, you don't have to succumb to his misogynistic insanity."

"Oh but Red, I like. I mean, I need it." She said as she continued towards The Joker. "It's a game, ain't that right Mister J."

"Yes, and I always win." He shot Ivy a glance of victory. "Now, Harley, purr for me."

She rolled her tongue seductively and stopped in front of him. She knelt down and waited for him to extend his hand before rising. Once again, he circled her body with his arms. He placed his fingers between her legs and rubbed her sex through her panties. She moaned in ecstasy as his other hand raked over her breasts.

Pamela looked away and backed against the wall. "If I can't get through to you, I guess I'll be leaving." Ivy turned to go to the door, but stopped when the Joker called out.

"Always took you for a coward."

"What do you mean 'coward?" She spun around.

"Your eyes reveal the truth. This turns you on, doesn't it? I bet you're nearly as wet as Harley, here." The Joker pushed Harley's panties and penetrated her in front of Pam. "If you ask nice, maybe Harl, would let you join in?"

He led Harley to the bedroom and Ivy couldn't help but follow. He locked the door behind them.

Pam couldn't take her eyes off the show. She couldn't stop her hand from falling to her side and then against the flesh of her thigh. She placed one leg over a vine and let it fall against her. A small moan escaped her as she desperately tried to stay focused.

"Oh pumpkin, look at your good friend Ivy. She wants to have some fun with us. Is that okay with you?" The Joker placed his fingers against her pussy and hit the spot instantly.

"Yes, ohhh yes,"

"You're in luck. Harley is in a sharing mood. So, tonight you get to be our little special guest star – our own little fuck toy."

Ivy didn't want to be turned on by him. He was a crude, evil demented man but she couldn't deny that the sex in the room was getting to her. She needed to leave.

"I'm nobody's fuck toy and I'm taking off." She turned to go but the Joker walked over to her and ran his body against hers. "I know you've had a few vines between your legs before, but I'm willing to bet you never had one like this."

She stayed against him but shook her head. "braggart."

"It's not bragging if it's true. You are hot, Ivy. I always thought that." He pulled her dress off in one tug and there she stood in a pair of green panties and a matching bra.

He stared her up and down and licked his lips. "Take your clothes off and get over here, Harley." He said in a demanding dark tone ensuring everyone knew who was in charge of this little game.

'Yes sir!" she said throwing her dress to the ground. She stood in front of both of them naked. The Joker moved in and kissed Harley hard. He then turned to Ivy and before she knew what was happening his tongue was in her mouth and she was kissing his back.

"Pammie go sit on the bed. We'll give you a little show first."

"No one tells me what to do." She said firmly.

"Fine, stand there. We'll take the bed. Harley get on the bed. Tonight, you play a virgin. Got it."

"I like that." She said coyly and then immediately went over to the bed and got under the covers as if she were nervous and it were her first time.

The Joker unbuttoned his suit jacket and pushed it to the floor. He unfastened his shirt and sat next to her. "So Harley-girl, tell me about yourself."

"Well, Mister J, it's just I've never been with anyone before. I'm scared."

"Poor thing, how far have you gone?"

"This one time, this guy kissed me and he tried to touch my chest, but I pushed him away."

"You mean no one has seen those beautiful breasts before?"

"No sir,"

"Well, that's a bad thing. When this guy kissed you did he use his tongue?"

"Ummm, he tried but I stopped kissing him."

"Such a good girl," he ran his finger down her bottom lip. "Do you want me to kiss you?"

Pammie was against the wall holding on to her vine and running it across her sex. This was like nothing she had seen before. Her head was telling her to get the hell out of there – that it was sexist- and wrong, but it was so intense.

"Can you show me how Mister J?"

"I'd be delighted. Open your mouth. Good girl," he moved in and slowly kissed her. He licked the inside of her mouth. She had to fight every instinct to pull him on top of her, but this was a game and she had to play by the rules.

"Now put your tongue in my mouth," she followed instruction and did her best to be clumsy, but every now and then, her body took over and she took control of his mouth. He grabbed hold of her wrist and she'd remember and slowed down.

"I want to see your breasts. Let daddy see your breasts."

Ivy was now penetrating herself with her hand. "Show him," she said aloud as the fight in her disappeared and lust took control.

She slowly dropped the sheet and lowered her head as if she were shy in the reveal. Harley was falling into the character. "Do they look okay?"

"They're perfect," Ivy said walking toward the bed still riding her hand.

He began raking his fingers over her tits.

"Do you touch your pussy, Harley?"

"Ummmm, no Mister J. I was told that was a dirty habit that made God angry."

"Yeah, but it feels so good. You want to feel good?" He removed the sheet and by this time Pamela was sitting on the edge of the bed.

"Yes, make me feel good."

"I can do that, but you'd be making God angry. I'd have to be your God."

'You are my God!" She said honestly as he kissed her hotly again.

"Lie back, Harley."

She did as he told. He got on top of her and took her hand. He pressed it against her sex.

"Oh, bad girl, you're all wet." He grinded his hard cock against her as he unbuckled his pants with his other hand. "Do you know what that is?"

"Yes," Harley said innocently.

"Say it. Say you want my cock."

"Oh God," she pushed against him and began circling her body around his. She felt his flesh. He took himself out of his pants. He was against her leg and refusing to move inside of her. "Come on, my own little virgin. Tell me to fuck you. Tell me you want my cock."

"Yes," Ivy was rocking her pussy, "Tell him. I want to watch."

"And hopefully join in," The Joker smiled at her. He leaned over and kissed her hard. She fell into it and let her tongue wander. She took control of the kiss and then broke away. "Fuck her," Ivy said. "Do it."

"Not until she begs. Beg me Harley." He took Ivy's arm and pressed it against Harley's sex. Harley pushed against her hand. Ivy delved her fingers into her and hit Harley's clit.

A tremor ran through her. The Joker shoved Pam's hand away. "Not yet. She hasn't begged for it yet. Beg daddy." He pulled both legs around him and placed his cock right at her center.

"I want it. I want your cock. I need it."

He grunted as he thrust into her full force, full length. She cried out in pleasured pain.

"More, More," She pushed back against him.

Pamela stretched out next to her and started rubbing her hands on Harley's breasts. "so beautiful" Ivy whispered. She licked Harley's nipple. She turned Harley's head to face her and kissed her hard.

The Joker kept thrusting as he watched the women caress each other. He pushed hard and hit the spot as Harley screamed out in pleasure. "MISTER J, MISTER J,"

He withdrew himself and turned to Ivy. "Your turn."

"Yeah, well, I'm not as complicit as Harley."

The Joker moved Harley aside and pushed Ivy down to the bed. His fully erect cock glistening from Harley's wetness pointed right at her. "You're our little fuck toy, remember."

"I'm nobody's toy."

"A challenge. I like that." He ran his cock against her panties.

Harley rolled over and had a huge smile on her face. "That was amazing."

"It always is. Here you go baby, kiss Pammie." He pushed Ivy towards her and Harley wrapped her arms around Ivy and kissed her.

Pamela groaned against the kiss as The Joker ran his hand on her rear and then pulled her against his lap as he sat up. She was now straddling him while Harley continued to lick her lips and nibble her neck.

"You are a good little whore," he said to Ivy who was too busy kissing Harley to protest. He ripped off her panties and unclasped her bra.

"I'm on top," Ivy said impaling herself on him. She was firm and tight.

"Not for long," he flipped her over and began fucking her hard.

"What do you want, Joker?" Ivy's heart was beating through her chest. She hated her body for reacting to him, but she couldn't help herself. She wanted to fuck Harley and damn it, she wanted to fuck The Joker too.

"I love those words out of your mouth. Let's start with you on your knees," He withdrew himself and stood up.

"Oh yes, Mister J!" Harley began penetrating herself on the bed. "Suck him, Ivy. Fuck her mouth, baby."

"You heard the lady,"

"Do it, Pam. Please. For me." Harley's grabbed a pillow and rode it to near climax. Her body was bouncing on the bed in anticipation.

Pam dropped to her knees. Face to face with his cock, she had to admit he was huge. "I didn't think you were packing this much heat," she admitted.

"I didn't tell you to speak." He shoved himself hard in her mouth as Harley groaned in ecstasy. She longed to watch The Joker thrust into Ivy's beautiful lips.

"Take it, Red. Take it." Harley couldn't help it anymore. She crawled off the bed and over to them. She stood above Ivy and looked at the Joker with lust in her eyes.

"Harder baby, fuck her harder." She kissed him hard on the lips while holding Ivy's head on him as he fucked her face.

He could feel himself on the brink and pulled himself out. "Not till I feel that tight pussy again," he said and picked Ivy up by the hair.

He threw her on the bed and was on top of her as Harley joined them. "You're so beautiful Red," she ran her hands over Ivy's hardened nipples. "Beg Mister J to fuck you," Harley spread Ivy's leg and pressed her wet pussy right against her friend's thigh. "I want to hear you beg him," she ran her wetness up and down.

The Joker teased Ivy's clit by pressing his cock against her.

"Okay, Oh God, fuck me. Please. Fuck me."

The Joker laughed and sank himself deep inside. He penetrated her over and over again and Ivy met every thrust. Harley licked and bit Ivy. She took Ivy's hand and put it on her wetness.

"There, and there," Harley rocked against Pam's fingers as The Joker kept thrusting. "Oh God, daddy, I need it. I need it."

The Joker pulled out of Ivy and within moments was in Harley's pussy hitting the spot. He came hard against her while her entire body pulsated.

"Sit up," He brought Harley to the edge of the bed and widened her legs. "Tell our little fuck toy to lick your pussy."

Harley was hit by an aftershock at his words. "Red, I want you to eat me." She said looking at The Joker whose entire chest was moving up and down. "Lick my pussy. Come on. Do it!" The more turned on Mister J got, the more forceful Harley got. "Come on, you want to be our little fuck toy. Come on."

Ivy couldn't help herself. She had wanted Harley for so long. It was a fantasy she had for months. She lowered herself and was on all fours in front of her. "You're amazing." Ivy whispered and then her mouth was on Harley.

Harley laid back on the bed and moved against Pam's mouth. She moved her pussy in circular motions, "that's it. You're just our fuck toy, Red. Oh god yes! You're a living fuck toy. Come on, use your tongue. Make her daddy. Make her use her tongue."

The Joker walked up behind Pam and raising her up with one thrust he was inside of her from the back. "Keep licking her," he shoved her head between Harley's legs. He felt Ivy climaxing as Harley tightened her legs around Pam.

He pushed once more sending sensations through Ivy's body. He came hard as Harley had orgasm after orgasm hit her.

After a few moments, The Joker stretched out on his bed. He tossed Ivy's dress at her. "That was fun," he said nonchalantly as Harley cuddled up to him.

"That was amazing. You are just amazing." She whispered to him, her fingers dancing on his cock. "Isn't he amazing?" Harley asked Pam who was straightening her dress and putting on her shoes.

"Pammie, you're being rude. Harley asked you a question."

She took a few breaths. Ran her fingers through her hair and shook her head. "Um, listen I'm leaving. This was a mistake. Don't mention it to anyone, ever."

She hurried out of the house causing The Joker to crack up laughing.

"What's up with that?" Harley asked.

"She can't handle it. She's a woman who thinks she always needs to have control to be in control. Her body wanted to be manhandled and fucked, but she doesn't want to think about that part of her. The animal in her."

"Why?"

"Because she aims to be a feminist but has no idea what it means. She thinks a feminist restricts you from letting go – giving power away. A true feminist – a true woman has the ability to do anything she wants – including letting a man be strong and forceful. Whatever you want, whatever you desire, just go for it. Don't put restrictions on yourself. You only live once and that's why I make the most of it. Laughing every moment. I have to say, you did surprise me. Letting Pammie in our little game."

"It was fun. Plus, if I ever thought you liked her better than me, I'd just kill her." Harley made a motion across her neck as if she would slice her.

"You definitely know how to hit a man's buttons. If only we didn't have a priest downstairs waiting to be killed."

"He can wait." She leaned in and kissed him hard. "Unless, you're not up for another round."

He grabbed her by the wrists, pushed her down and got on top of her. He took her thigh in his hand and pushed hard into her. "I'm always up for another round." He jammed himself into her fast and quick bringing them both to a hot climax. She trembled against him as she came.

"Before we kill this priest, what do you say we have him make you my wife."

"Oh God, yes. YES!" She hugged him. "I have to pick out something to wear!"

"Okay dollface, just make it fast." She rose from the bed, he hit her on the rear and laughed. "Money, power, and destroying Batman – this is the life."

PART 3

HARLEY QUINN BREAKS FROM A LIFE OF CRIME.

CHAPTER 01

The age old saying that was repeated on every commercial, cartoon, PSA, comic book, and safety pamphlet for God knows how long. It was common knowledge that in this day and age, going against the law almost always ended bad for you, especially when superheroes got involved and laid you the fuck out in broad daylight. It just wasn't worth it sometimes.

But it certainly paid better than sitting on your ass doing nothing.

Harley Quinn, former arm candy of the infamous Joker himself, was at a crossroads. With Joker's latest scheme going up in smoke, and the clown prince getting his ass thrown into Arkham again for the umpteenth time, Harley wasn't looking good on the financial front. They spent most of their money on their "master plan" and with no reward for their risk, all they got was the typical Batman ass-whooping that usually came with the deal, and Harley was in dire straits. Obviously, her first thought was to get a job, but she was hardly business savvy and she time as a therapist had soured somewhat thanks to her "initiation" by the

Joker himself-not to mention her skin was deathly pale and she was crazier than whoever voted for president.

What Harley needed was a place where a young and beautiful woman like her could work and make some money without attracting the Dark Knight on her fine ass. Someplace that could overlook her physical appearance (which she could easily play off as "I'm a victim of the Joker" and get tons of sympathetic looks and pats on the back).

A strip club. Yup, not the first place you'd think for a former villain but it was the only place where she could lay low and make good use of her "goods". Girls passed in an out all the time, all money exchanges happened under the table without anything scary like taxes hanging over them, and Batman probably didn't even go near places like that (Harley had a feeling he was more into the fetish range of things with all that leather he had on. Maybe S&M). And she was insanely hot, as many of her secret fans online mentioned a couple of hundred times in her defense.

It was all too easy getting a spot in this little strip club called Juggles, which, ironically, had nothing to do with juggling. It was a bit weird at first getting dressed up as a sexy schoolgirl or police officer and then stripping it all off for a crowd of horny pervs, but she had the physique for it, and the flexibility. Her first dance was a hit and she already had men eating out of the palm of her hand. She even scored her first private session with one of the boys, and that was when she decided to throw caution to the wind and rake up some more dough for herself.

"That's right, tiger, you just hit the jackpot!" Pushing her ample chest into the young man's face, Harley got direct and wicked in what she was doing, straddling his lap and teasing her cock with her hands. "Those other sluts don't know how to run this joint, but I'm gonna show you how I do things around here!"

If there was one thing that Harley liked about Juggles, it was the flexibility of what a girl could do to make money. It was all up to the girl to determine how far they could go in this line of work. The more morally flexible you are, the more you stand to gain. And considering her financial troubles, Harley was willing to put a lot out there, even when it came to essentially whoring herself out in the private rooms of a strip club.

Harley sank to her knees, and she was pleasantly surprised at how big her client's cock was. The guy was in his early twenties, clearly new to the whole stripping business, but he was definitely packing some heat. She grasped the base of his cock and started to stroke it while she brought licks and adoring kisses along the length of his cock.

"Let's start with my mouth first, before we move onto my tits. You seem like a guy who could use a little prep work." Harley grinned coyly.

Harley wasn't the type of girl who had the patience to play coy here. She wanted to earn her money and get out of her money troubles. She never imagined herself actually giving into sex for money, but she found it far easier to do than she thought. Maybe it was the thought that if she did well enough with this horny fuck, then she could attract customers with even bigger pockets. Harley was determined now, eager to give up fully to this incredibly odd situation she ran headfirst in and would deal with the consequences later.

So she took his cockhead into her mouth, very abrupt in how she began to suck him in deep, hand holding around his base and jerking it steadily, providing a limit to how far she could go. He throbbed within the embrace of her grip and her mouth, and she knew she had him where she wanted him, and that he would stay there. She pressed on bolder, stronger, giving herself fully to this weirdness as she took him on carefully, drawing back to lavish him with licks and kisses. It was ecstatic and excessive, a show of chaos and hunger almost too weird and hot even for her, but Harley had no hang-ups here and no reason to resist.

"You're amazing." The man groaned, the eagerness and enthusiasm behind Harley's indulgence of his bod driving him wild. He didn't expect the new girl at the club to be so good at her first time. And the fact that she looked like Harley Quinn (hottest villain in his opinion) only made the experience even hotter.

Harley sucked and stroked his cock until it was all nice and slick, until she had thoroughly prepared and treated him, at which point the former villain went right into something bigger, shoving forward as she pushed her chest against his lap and grasped her ample tits firmly, pushing them together and moving fluidly into a titfuck with such confidence that it startled her client.

"Told ya you needed to be prepared." She laughed.

He couldn't help but agree as he felt the amazing embrace of Harley's big tits wrapped around his shaft, heaving up and down with the confidence and firmness of a woman on a mission. Harley didn't have the time, patience, or control to be anything other than ready to satisfy him, and she put one of her best assets to work in tending to his cock now, desperate and firm in her approach. His lecherous gaze made her feel warm and excited, and it increased her growing enjoyment of this lewd activity.

The money had already been arranged, laying on the sugar and the sex was just a matter of completing the transaction, but Harley found it rather freeing; she didn't have to worry about whether or not there would be work, not worry about if she would be able to stand up the next morning after one of Joker's "fits", here she could just go on and enjoy the benefits of pre-arranged success. It was a nice change of pace for her, not having to worry about getting thrown into the crazy bin again. It all had her melting into the throes of excitement and heat that she was happy to tend to. And with how big this man's cock was, she could even lean down and suck on the head while she kept the pace up with her chest, adding another dimension to the pleasure.

The man's cock throbbed under her touch, and Harley felt like she was really hitting her stride in all this, like she was bringing it all together perfectly. This little cock sucking session was getting too hot for words to describe, and her client's moans kept her moving stronger, quicker, more firmly as she satisfied all of his urges and desires. It was so much that Harley shot her head down into the cock sticking out of her cleavage and took a nice, long suck, as if she were trying to inhale his dick all at once.

Harley's suction technique was more than enough to drive her customer over the edge. He groaned and gasped, pleasure seizing hold of him and overwhelming him as he gave it all up. His cock erupted suddenly, gushing thick shots of stick spun all over the tops of her breasts, leaving her feeling like an overwhelmed and eager mess now. She took it all in stride of course, for despite how strange and out of control she had gotten, Harley was still equipped to handle madness of all kinds.

Harley would be lying if she said that she didn't feel a tiny ounce of shame at sucking dick for money on top of being a stripper. A part of her wondered what Joker would think of her. Well, she quickly rationalized that Joker was living it up with his psychopathic peeps in Arkham while she was hanging on the edge of getting evicted and begging for scraps. She was doing what she had to do to survive, nothing more. Not like he had a clown budget to fall back on anyway.

Word spread quickly, and soon she had a fairly decent selection of men willing to spend a lot of money with a lot of time with the new girl on the block. Some of them she turned down because they just weren't her style, but most paid good money to give her the sort of attention she, to be perfectly honest, had never gotten from Joker. In just two weeks since her first private dance she had already paid off her rent and gotten herself a small television to make the place seem decent for once.

She set up a schedule over the next few months, stripping at night and meeting clients during the day. Harley began setting actual prices for her services; blowjobs were the cheapest, followed by the full service that included both her mouth and pussy. Her audience was broad and varied, but there were a few regulars that had taken a strong liking to her. Among them was a young man named Frank.

Frank was one of those elite, smug rich snobs who went to private academies that Gotham loved to glorify to draw attention away from the fact that the city was a fucking nightmare. When Harley first saw him, she wasn't impressed; slightly disheveled hair, short, a bit chubby...he looked like he was barely past eighteen and probably didn't know how to fuck. She almost handed him a lollipop and patted his head before telling him to piss off before he waved an envelope full of crisp hundred dollar bills that she knew from sight alone went up into the thousands. She knew she couldn't refuse that much money, and judging from the smug look on his face, he knew that too.

Frank knew what he was getting into, he even booked a room at a fancy hotel where they could fuck in luxury. After counting the money, Harley went forth to show him what Gotham's number one whore could do, only to freeze at the sight of his cock. It was big, too big. And what's worse is that he knew exactly how to use it.

Harley gasped as she was thrown onto the bed, with Frank's large naked body climbing after her as he squeezed her large breasts in a greedy grasp. She moaned as his fingers sank into her soft, warm flesh, and he grinned wide as he got into position between her legs.

'Jesus criminiy, Batman, what do these rich snobs teach their kids at home?!' Harley thought startled as Frank lifted her legs and tore off her thong. His big, heavy cock slapped down on her pussy before lining up and shoving inside caring nothing for hesitation as he plunged himself in. Harley's eyes went crossed as Frank started to fuck her. His arms locked around her legs to keep her half suspended and his steadily slammed forward, filling the room with wet, loud slaps.

Harley stared at the ceiling, her eyes watering and mouth agape, forced to contend with getting fucked hard by a kid who by rights shouldn't even know what tits feel like. He slammed in so deep and stretched her cunt so completely that it struck places she didn't even know she had, and it made her toned thighs shiver in desire. As the pleasure finally reached her brain, she reached forward and wrapped her arms around his neck, panting and moaning like the wanton whore she was.

"T-That's right...fuck me, you...you fat bastard!" She howled. Her legs stretched out and hitched against his sides, holding onto him harder and harder. She was about to order him to make her cum, when she did just that, her eyes rolling back in her head as she squirted against his lap. It was a violent first orgasm that left their laps damp, and yet Frank showed no signs of stopping. What the hell was he made of?!

Harley had no idea how long he pounded his cock into her like that. All that she knew was that she came again and again from it. The entire time it remained stiff and ferociously thick for what felt like hours; he was the largest she had ever encountered by far, and the entire time Frank held himself back from cumming. He wanted to completely dominate her, to let her know that despite how many men she's fucked, he will always be the best she'd ever had. And Harley completely agreed with that belief.

It wasn't until Harley was a shivering mess of pleasure and sweat that Frank decided she had earned her reward—a thick load of creamy, Gotham elite cum. Harley just lied there on her back, her hair undone and spread across the sheets, her pale white face red and sweaty, her big breasts bouncing on every thrust and sporting more than just a few slap marks. He pinched her nipples to get her attention as Frank neared his peak.

"Here it comes, whore." He grinned and licked his lips. Harley was convinced he had to be some kind of metahuman. Seriously, the guy barely looked tire! Somehow that thought made it easier to accept that she had been fucked senseless by this chubby little stud with the cock attitude. "Get ready...you're getting all my cum!"

He pulled back and drilled his cock down one more time into her depths. Her strong thighs wrapped around his waist and kept him trapped, locking behind his back so that he wouldn't be able to peel himself away any time soon. As Frank's head rolled back, his cock unleashed a torrent of cum that filled her more than she ever imagined, a wash of stick, warm cream rushing inside her and filling her entire body with a soothing sensation. Harley howled and screamed, her fingers gripping his shoulders tightly, and she was hit by the biggest orgasm she ever had with a client.

Harley was nearly catatonic when Frank finally pulled his cock out, watching as her pussy immediately leaked an enormous amount of cream onto the bed. When she regained consciousness, Harley would quickly find herself burning Frank's number into her mind as she hugged the massive stack of bills to her chest in glee.

Before she knew it, Harley Quinn had gotten used to her new life as a stripper and prostitute. Not only did she have a solid fanbase at the strip club, she also started making friends with the other girls, who soon started to see her as some idol and rising star. Her daytime clients varied from young studs who used her as a cocksleeve to married men looking for release and businessmen looking for a good time. There were even some women, for whom she gave a discount if they brought their own toys.

It wasn't a surprise that Harley was rented out by some guys looking to celebrate their Friday night with a good old gang bang. Harley rarely did gang bangs, but she certainly didn't complain when she saw the money they were offering her. Harley may be insane, but her mother didn't raise no fool.

"Come on in, boys, the Harlequin is open for business!" Harley hollered as she shifted in one young man's lap, a hand on his cock. He was young enough to be a recent high school graduate, but that hardly mattered to her. He also had a very thick package that was just eager to get into her pussy. "I'm not the usual teenage hottie that you boys usually go for, but I can certainly rock your world better than those other sluts!"

There wasn't much subtlety in her advance, not that she needed any, as the three college students crowded around her with the intent to fuck her without abandon and get their money's worth. The second student grasped her hips and came up behind her, while the tallest of the three, a soccer player with a large upper body, stepped in toward her lips. All three were considerably gifted, and were very eager in wanting to have their way with her. Which she encouraged wholeheartedly.

Guiding the first man's cock into her first, she took her time with this, as the second began to pump steadily into her ass and the third ran his fingers through her pigtails and guided his tip toward her lips. There was no shame in the mutual advance everyone gave into, accepting the pleasure and excitement that soon ensued amid the swell of lustful confidence guiding Harley into her task. Three men at once. She wouldn't have ever imagined she was capable of this, but she wanted it now more than she could handle, craving the idea of pushing herself to her absolute limits in sluttiness and letting them do whatever they wanted to her.

Three big cocks sinking into her body was a dream come true for Harley, and she couldn't contain her excitement, moaning louder and stronger as she rocked back and forth in needy, approving delight. Everything she did was an expression of her winding appetites now, a show of hunger and lust taking her on as she worked in the motions greedily. The boys took her at once, filling her holes and patiently fucking her, letting the tension build, and Harley had to wonder how often they did this. With how smoothly they worked in tandem in taking her, this couldn't have been the first time they fucked a woman at once.

Not that such an idea bothered Harley. This pleasure was too potent and fierce for her to have any concerns of that sort. She was shameless about giving herself too this pleasure fully, feeling the differences in how the students had their way with her as the sensations began to rise up and they fell into their patterns. One young man from below thrust up into Harley with a steadiness and firmness that showed he was happy letting her take change, having plenty of time to grope and play with her heaving breasts. The second student, seemingly eager to impress his two friends, fucked Harley's ass with deep strokes and a firm speed that sorely lacked confidence, making up for it with gusto and firmness instead. The sports student, with his fingers entangled in Harley's hair, gripping her pigtails as he fucked her mouth in shallow strokes, never going too hard or too rough, a consummate gentleman even with his balls slapping against her chin.

There was a lot going on here that left Harley dizzy. The idea of having three men younger than her fucking her holes, treating her like a sex toy to happily indulge in, was something that she would not have thought possible, but now it was all that she craved, urging her to buck on stronger and needier to satisfy these three without hesitation. To suck on the cock pumping into her throat while her hips thrashed between the cock in her cunt and the shaft impaling her bowels. There was a lot going on at once, and she felt capable of dealing with all of it now, invincible and bold in her pursuit of carnal delights. There was so much to enjoy and so little time to give up to all of it.

The sweet groans of men loving the pleasures of Harley Quinn's perfect body only further excited her. Everything she did involve something brilliant, something hot, and she couldn't slow down. She needed to get fucked, cement her new life as a successful whore. It made her head spin, but she still pushed on, showing off her sexual prowess and her willingness to abandon everything now for the sake of these appetites.

Her strng work ethic even in the face of bliss and delirium brought her the validation she craved, as the three students lost themselves to her body's seductive delights in one fell stroke. Cocks pushed deep into her, throbbing and pulsing with the thrill of salty bliss, giving Harley so much cum to enjoy and savor, an eager mess sucking it all down and embracing her climax. She took all this in stride, her own orgasm surging through her as they pumped her full of cum, rewarding her with the thrill of something so powerful and relieving that she couldn't imagine not wanting this.

In the end of it all Harley felt like a queen. Sure, she was a queen who spent half her time on her back with her legs spread in the air, but at least she wasn't in jail with her nearly-forgotten boyfriend. The more time she spent dancing, stripping, and fucking, the more her old life faded into the background, replaced by the current version of herself: a financially stable, widely adored and blissfully happy young woman.

All it took was transitioning from a crazy clown villain to a submissive whore. Honestly, it was no different from what she did as Joker's arm candy, only without the violence and constant fear. If she'd known it was this much fun, she'd done it years ago.

It was a happy and fulfilling life for Harley Quinn, and she wouldn't have it any other way.

THE END......

AUTHOR NOTE

Thank you for reading this story, I hope you enjoyed it as much as i did writing it for you. The concluding part of the story will be in the next edition of this book attached to it as a series, hopefully, it would have been released by the time you are reading this. I will really love ur feedback so i will have my eyes on my email inbox, so , therefore, please kindly use the comment section of where you purchased this book from to place your reviews, suggestion and ratings for this book for it will help me improve the forth coming stories that are yet to be released. You can contact me the author via my email (lifeisg00d@gmx.us).